As she listens to the horrors that Alice and Sasha endured at the hands of their captors, Kathy realizes she has to know, she MUST know everything Alice has been up to. She wants to understand what kept them apart these past years...beyond her own anger at what her wife is capable of.

As the gruesome details of Alice and Sasha's story unfold, Kathy asks herself 'Does this justify what they did and are doing to those people? Does it explain their prolonged absence from their families?'

Follow along as Alice and Sasha go in for the kill! Learn how they carefully plot their revenge against the people who took so much from their lives...and take just as much and more from them in return.

Their lives, their victims' lives, will never be the same!

A K'Anne Meinel Novella

Videos

Biography of Books
Ships
Sapphic Surfer
Ghostly Love
Long Distance Romance
Germanic
Sensual Sapphic

Sapphic Cowgirl
Couples
Lie Next To Me
Sapphic Cowboi
Timed Romance
Readings (SHIPS)

K'ANNE MEINEL

Meddlesome

Malice

ISBN-13: 978-0692720400
ISBN-10: 0692720405

K'Anne Meinel is available for comments at KAnneMeinel@aim.com as well as on Facebook, Google +, or her blog @ http://kannemeinel.wordpress.com/ or on Twitter @ kannemeinelaim.com, or on her website @ www.kannemeinel.com if you would like to follow her to find out about stories and book's releases.

www.shadoepublishing.com

ShadoePublishing@gmail.com

Shadoe Publishing is a United States of America company
Cover by: K'Anne Meinel
Edited by: Deb Amia

PUBLISHER'S NOTE
This is a work of fiction. Names, characters, places, and incidents are the product of the author's imagination or are used fictitiously, and any resemblance to actual persons, living or dead, business establishments, events, or locales is entirely coincidental.
The publisher does not have any control over and does not assume any responsibility for author or third-party Web sites or their content.

Meddlesome ~ Fond of meddling, interfering.

"Maybe I should gloss over some of this?" Alice asked, thoughtfully.

"No, tell me everything. Don't leave out the details," Kathy answered with a gulp. Some of the 'details' were a bit much, but she knew she could handle it. This was only the tip of the iceberg. "I *need* to know," she pleaded. She needed to know why Alice had been gone so long. She needed to know everything....

Kathy couldn't remember a night where she had wanted the kids to go to bed so early since they were much younger. The teens seemed to sense she wanted them out of her hair and deliberately took their time.

"What'd you do today?" she was asked.

Her deliberately vague answer of, "Oh, this and that," wasn't enough to satisfy them. As teens, they felt they should be treated as adults and included in all adult decisions. Kathy couldn't very well explain to them that she had spent the day talking to their other mother, Alice. After all, Alice was supposedly dead.

The phone rang and Emily answered it. "Mom, it's Portia," she called out clearly.

As Kathy was doing the dishes, she called back, "Tell her I will have to call her back." She didn't want to talk to her friend. Portia, a lawyer, would immediately know something was up. They were already dealing with a lot of business and taxes and she just didn't want to cope with it at the moment. She wanted to know where Alice had been and what she had been doing. Alice would be able to solve the mess they found themselves in. She just knew that Alice could do anything.

Kathy heard Em tell Portia, "She's doing the dishes and asks if she can call you back...uh huh...yeah, I will. Bye." She hung up. "Portia says to call her when you can," she told her mother.

Kathy breathed a sigh of relief. She knew she only had a small window of time before Portia or Andie showed up at the house. While Alice was fairly well hidden, she didn't want to push her luck. She wanted to be alone so that Alice could tell her what had happened. She *needed* to know.

"Mom!" Sean practically yelled to get her attention.

Kathy started at the loud voice. "What?" she came back in a tone that told him she didn't appreciate his rude shouting.

"I've been trying to get your attention for a while," he pointed out contritely.

Kathy knew she had drifted off. She'd have to watch that. "What did you need?" she asked in a softer, more welcoming tone.

"You have to sign off on this paper," he explained.

Immediately suspicious, Kathy dried her hands, wondering if he was failing some course. She was delightfully surprised to see the A- on the paper he handed her. "An A minus," she said with pleasure. "Good for you!" she told him.

"Yeah, you were right. It wasn't so bad once I started the course," he said with a grin. He'd hated the course at the beginning of the year, but Kathy had insisted he couldn't drop it and he hadn't. Once he applied himself, it had worked out and he enjoyed what he was learning. He was doubly glad he wouldn't have to take it in college.

The kids did their homework and Kathy swore the time went by slower and slower as she impatiently waited through the homework, then their TV shows. She hoped she didn't glance too many times back at the room where she knew Alice was hiding, probably listening to her family enjoy time together without her.

"I'm going to bed," Sean finally announced when his show was over. "Remember, I'm staying after school tomorrow to play basketball," he reminded Kathy.

"Of course," she murmured, but she hadn't remembered at all.

"Can I stay and watch?" Em asked before Sean could give his mother a good night kiss.

"Why?" he asked, the older teen annoyed by his pesky sister.

She shrugged. "I just want to watch," she said in a tone that didn't convince either her mother or her brother.

"But why?" he asked.

"Well, you are my ride home," she pointed out, hoping to get him away from the real reason she wanted to stay after school to watch the basketball game.

Deciding not to tease her—after all she had been pretty sick earlier this year—he let her off the hook. Shrugging, he answered, "I don't care." He then leaned over to give Kathy a kiss good night on the cheek. "Night, Mom," he told her with a smile as he gathered his things and headed up the

stairs. For a second he thought he heard something and stopped, but when it wasn't repeated he continued on.

"So why do you really want to stay after school?" Kathy asked, astutely. Emily wasn't one to hang around her brother; they both had their own set of friends.

"Well, some of those guys have girlfriends who are on the pep squad…" she began, feeling herself blush at the news.

"You want to be on the pep squad next year?" Kathy asked, surprised. Emily was so frail still, but she was slowly coming back from the illness that had nearly killed her.

"Actually, I'd like to be a cheerleader. Could I, maybe, go to a camp or something?" she asked, hopefully.

Kathy thought about it for a moment. "Why don't you check out what's available? Are any of your friends going?" She knew that could be a big motivator to teens at this age. If their friends went, they went.

"No. No one else wants to be on the squad," she confessed sadly. Then, brightening up, she said, "But you always said I should be a leader not a follower."

Kathy smiled. It was always amusing when the kids used her own words against her. It was actually Alice who had said those exact words, but she wouldn't correct the young teen. "You are right," she told her instead. "C'mon, give me a hug and kiss good night," she told her.

After duly giving her mother a hug and a kiss, Emily pulled back to look at her mother. "Mom?" she began sadly. "Do you still miss Mom?"

Kathy knew exactly what the teen meant. Smiling, this time without the immediate tears that would normally have engendered, she answered. "Yes, I will always miss Mom," she told her truthfully. She was certain Alice was listening. She too had heard the noise that had stopped Sean on the steps.

"Think she's looking out for us?" Emily sounded like a little girl at the moment.

"She's always looking out for us," Kathy answered truthfully, because...she was.

Emily brightened up at this even further. It was nice that Mom didn't cry at the mention of their other mom. She missed Alice. She had been stern and some of her friends were frightened by her, but she had always been loving and Emily had known that she loved her. She missed her. She had understood so much. Not that Kathy didn't, but it wasn't the same...it would never be the same. "Good night, Mom," she said, giving her another hug and a kiss.

Kathy squeezed her little girl. She'd almost lost her, she'd almost died. Coming back from that wasn't easy and she knew being a teen was doubly hard. She almost wished she could send the teen into the spare bedroom to see her other mom, to heal, but it wasn't time yet. Alice needed to tell her where she had been and what had happened. "Good night, baby," she said in reply. She watched as Emily made her way upstairs. She sighed, gathering the teen's things that she had left in the TV room, otherwise tomorrow she'd leave them and not have them for school. Emily wasn't quite as neat as Sean, but maybe it was the illness, maybe it was the age difference, she wasn't sure.

Kathy felt, rather than saw, when Alice was standing there watching her. It gave her a warm tingly feeling that only this woman had ever managed to create inside her. Dating another woman had never caused the fluttering that began inside her stomach and could, with the right kisses and caresses, flutter out to her extremities. She knew she loved this woman, even if she was a serial killer. She knew she too had killed, but never to the extent that this woman had. That this woman loved her, she

had no doubt, but could she still live with all the killings Alice had done, even more than she knew of? There was only one way to find out.

"Are you hungry?" she asked her.

"Yeah, those pork chops you had smelled delicious," Alice told her.

"I'll heat you up a plate," Kathy told her as she finished gathering Emily's things to put by the front door.

"You okay?" Alice asked as she walked by her.

Kathy stopped to look at the blonde, examining her again. She couldn't get over the physical changes. She should look older, but the weight loss made her look younger. Only the eyes were exactly the same. At the moment they told Kathy that Alice did indeed love her. "Yes, everything is fine," she said quietly.

On impulse, Alice leaned in, hoping Kathy would meet her halfway. She was pleased when their lips met in a nice, warm kiss. Nothing passionate, just a good, loving kiss. She smiled as Kathy smiled back and then headed up the stairs. Alice watched her walk, admiring her buttocks and the way they swayed in the slacks she was wearing. Kathy had a small, middle-age spread, but Alice liked that about her. To Alice, Kathy was beautiful.

Kathy soon returned with a plate with two pork chops on it, a baked potato, green beans, and applesauce. On the side was a Seagram's flavored beer in black cherry that she knew Alice would enjoy.

"Oh, thank you. That smells wonderful," Alice told her. She began to eat as Kathy cleaned up the TV room, not that there was much to straighten up. "Am I making you nervous?" she asked around a pork chop as she pulled the meat from it with her teeth.

"No," Kathy answered and then looked straight at her wife, "I'm just wondering what else you have to tell me?"

Alice looked sad. "None of it is good," she promised quietly. "I'm not proud of what I did, but I had to do it."

Kathy understood. Alice had always justified the killings. There had just simply been too many of them over the years and Kathy knew she didn't even know the count. She often wondered if Alice knew. She shrugged philosophically. "I still want to know what happened."

Alice nodded. "Do you want to know now or..." she gestured at the food she was still eating.

"No, finish your meal. It can wait."

~ ~ ~ ~ ~

Leaving the small estate, Alice headed back to the shed where they changed into their own clothes, moved the man—after much wrestling—back to his own car and cut the bindings that held him. Leaving his car as much like they found it as they could, they sped off in their own and headed east instead of south. They had agreed that their time was up near and around St. Petersburg. They slept in the car that night in some out-of-the-way woods far from the road so they wouldn't be spotted. Still, they both felt that at any moment they would be discovered.

Alice drove them east for a while and then southeast towards Cherpovets. They checked into a decent hotel and were able to find a nice place to eat. Both of them were very hungry at this point. Alice sent Sasha out to do some shopping for dry goods while she fired up their laptop...something they could keep in the car to eat at any time or for snacks. The signal in this hotel was much better than any they had gotten in the smaller hotels they stayed in. She briefly wondered if the woman

she had left in their last hotel had been found yet, or the man she had knocked out, then, she dismissed them. She had other work to do.

The keylogger program allowed her to remotely access the computer they had been logged onto the previous night. It would send reports to her email address that she had set up specifically for this purpose. She began to go over the things Sasha had downloaded and was frustrated how much of it was in Russian script. What she could read in French and English though was enough for her to convict those people. She wanted to go back. She wanted to burn that house to the ground so it could all be over and she could return to her family. She was sick of this game they were playing already. The amounts she was seeing weren't just thousands here and there, but tens of thousands and upwards of millions of rubles, pounds, and dollars, as well as francs and deutschmarks and even euros. These people were into a lot of things that made Alice angry. From wholesale land grabbing to human slavery, from manufacturing of chemicals to owning factories where people worked for nearly nothing. She wondered if what she couldn't read in Russian was worse.

By the time Sasha returned with their groceries and a totally inadequate amount of food, Alice was pretty deep into the computer and what they had copied. Alice looked up for a moment, trying to remember why Sasha was there and then saw the groceries and got up.

"There's a lot for you to read through," she indicated the computer.

"Ya, does it tell us–" she began and was cut off when Alice swore.

"Brie? What the hell are we going to do with brie?" she asked, disgusted. She knew that Sasha hadn't shopped for herself in years, but a cheese like brie wasn't going to sustain them. She hated that she had to go everywhere with Sasha to make sure things were done right.

"I thought…" Sasha began in defense of herself and then stopped. She knew anything she said to Alice wouldn't matter. She knew she knew

nothing about 'common' living. Used to the best, used to years of being spoiled and having people to do things for her, she was a mess. "I'm sorry," she finished softly.

Alice took a deep breath. Blaming Sasha for the bad groceries wasn't going to solve the problem. She vowed to go with the Russian once or twice more to show her what she meant when she said 'snacks' and 'dry foods.' Where the hell were they going to put frozen concentrate? She looked around the hotel room, it didn't even have a small refrigerator. She decided to make it instead, using the ice pitcher that they did have.

Meanwhile, Sasha had sat down to read what Alice had been looking at. She found several transactions that involved property that had been owned by her or her father. This went back many years. The Assemblage had been working for years, not just on the Brenhov holdings, but many others as well. Sasha could feel the slow burn of her anger building.

"Dis doesn't show vhat they ordered to be done to me," she said angrily, slapping a hand towards the laptop.

"No, but you can see where they went after you and yours. That's where we begin," Alice said as she mixed the can of juice with water.

"Dey can't really tink dey vill get avay vith dis?"

"They have," Alice said drily as she poured each of them a glass of juice. Handing one to Sasha, she sat down in the room's only other chair and took a sip. "We have to decide, do we go solely after The Assemblage or do we go after them and their families...the whole works?"

Sasha stared at her in horror as she realized what Alice was implying. She quickly spoke up, "Only dose involved in De Assemblage."

Alice nodded, glad to know Sasha wasn't bloodthirsty. "You know, if we had started last night, half of those people," she nodded towards the computer, "would already be gone."

Sasha looked from Alice to the people on the spreadsheet she was reading, who had been paid and who now owned properties throughout the world for The Assemblage. She knew that using legal means would not only take years, but would probably be mostly unsuccessful. These people did not play by the rules. Neither could Sasha. "How do ve take dem out?"

Alice was pleased, but didn't show it. "I'd like to take out as many as possible at one time. Once word gets out that we are targeting members of The Assemblage, they will hire bodyguards and go hide. We should keep compiling dossiers on every one of them, as well as their family members. You can't tell me that those people," she interrupted Sasha from going off about the families, "don't know or don't inherit once these others are out of the way."

"So ve kill dem all?" she asked, horrified.

Alice shook her head. "Worse! We bankrupt them all. We only kill those directly associated with or part of The Assemblage."

Sasha breathed an inward sigh of relief as she nodded. That was something she could live with. She took a drink of juice and then looked at the glass. "Dis stuff is terrible," she commented.

"Yes, yes it is," Alice agreed with a grin and still she drank it.

Sasha lifted her glass in salute to Alice.

~ ~ ~ ~ ~

They stayed in Cherpovets for a full week as they compiled more data from the computer information they had lifted. It seemed each time they found more information it spiderwebbed into an even bigger web of deceit, theft, extortion, and corruption. These people weren't like the mob, and yet they were bigger, their goals were bigger, their money was more

extensive. They used the mob as their plaything. Alice was quite alarmed as she realized the scope. They wouldn't be going home anytime soon and this distressed her and angered her. She wanted to begin to take action, but she knew that she must first plan it out or they would get caught. Then they would be arrested and either killed or sent to a worse prison than what they had been in. She wanted revenge, but justifiable revenge.

~ ~ ~ ~ ~

"I think I need to go work for these people," Alice indicated two on the list, a husband and wife 'team' who seemed to be at the heart of The Assemblage, which they were still trying to figure out. It seemed to have branches within branches and those directly responsible for the attack on Sasha were hard to figure out. If they killed them one at a time, it would take ages. It would also alert the others, and that they did not want.

"How can you?" Sasha asked, concerned.

"One, I think we should both be black-haired and you wear your glasses. I think this will really throw off anyone looking for the two blondes who escaped from Honduras. Two, the redheads up in St. Petersburg and Vereya are long gone too. If you could befriend this person," she pointed to the sub-heading picture under one of their suspects, "you could probably get a job, but you are going to have to act like a servant. Do you think you can do that?"

Sasha looked indignant and then she thought about what Alice was saying. Used to having servants all her life, she wasn't certain she could act like one. She hadn't noticed them. They had just always been there. "I guess I could…" she began hesitantly.

"Look, these aren't things we can screw up," Alice told her exasperatedly. "Once you get in, you can get me in and I'll take care of some of the things you don't know or won't know to look for." Alice drilled her for hours, asking pertinent questions, trying to get her to forget her elitist past.

Sasha was surprised what Alice knew and how to execute it. She laughed with her over her own foibles, she hadn't realized how upper crust she had become. She actually came from very humble beginnings so she should be able to do this.

They found a sublet for the duration of their stay in Vologda, where their intended victims lived. It was a nice house in an historic area. Vologda was known for its administrative, cultural, and scientific people. Sasha took pride in showing Alice around the beautiful city. It was a central city with transportation in the form of the federal highway, trains, and buses all coming through. It was a historical city with over two hundred nationally recognized historical monuments. Alice was enjoying the beauty of it, but never forgot why they really were there. She practiced her Russian and halting as it was, the people were fascinated by this French ex-patriot that was now living in their city. They believed her and that was paramount to their anonymity. Sasha too was pretending to be from another country.

The real test came the next day when Sasha 'happened' to meet up with Anya Koslowski in the park where she was walking a baby in a stroller. She sat down at the bench that Alice had observed the woman sitting at daily.

"Hello," she said in a pleasant voice and pretended an interest in the baby. "What a beautiful baby. Is it yours?"

Anya, pleased by the interest and proud of her position as nanny for the Bogomolov family, was easy to obtain information from. As Alice had

taught her, it wasn't much different than negotiating a contract, getting your business associates to tell you more than you told them. "Oh you are looking for work? I'm sure I could recommend you," she told Sasha in a friendly voice. She was pleased to help and make a new friend.

Willow Wentworth appeared promptly at 9 a.m. on the Bogomolov doorstep the next day. Anya had promised her an interview and Sasha had given her the phone number to confirm.

"How do you do?" the butler answered the door.

"Very well, thank you," Sasha, aka Willow answered politely and modestly as Alice had directed. "I have an appointment with Mrs. Bogomolov at 9 a.m.? I am Willow Wentworth."

"Ah yes, if you would come in please," he said loftily, exerting his place without trying. Even among servants there was a hierarchy.

Sasha was led into the old townhome that had been masterfully restored. It spoke of opulence, it spoke of class, but most of all it spoke of money. As she kept her demeanor humble, she was pleased to meet with Mrs. Bogomolov who spent the time talking about herself and her family, never questioning Sasha's qualifications. Sasha, or rather Willow, got the job as a maid. She was thrilled and actually seemed enthusiastic about starting the job, which impressed Mrs. Bogomolov. They made arrangements for her to get a uniform the following day and start later that day.

"Do be sure to come to the back door tomorrow," the butler warned her as he let her out.

"Good for you!" Alice praised her. She'd spent the day walking about the city, getting the feel for it, hopelessly lost for a while, but even that was to her benefit should they need it.

Sasha was a bit pleased with herself for getting the job. She had no clue what exactly she would be doing as a maid, but Alice assured her someone would show her and all she had to do was do it well. Later, she could start her observations and eventually introduce Alice into the household as a friend from France who had decided to start over in Vologda.

Sasha was shocked to realize how much work a maid did, but she didn't complain. In fact, she kept to herself and listened to the other servants. Besides a butler, there was a cook, another maid, the nanny, Anya, and several temps who came in for various functions. The Bogomolovs liked to entertain. Sasha was shocked when she recognized a couple of their visitors. She kept herself as unobtrusive as possible and fortunately for her the other maid, who had seniority over Willow, the new maid, was the one to wait upon the visitors.

"They are having a party," Sasha informed Alice a couple of weeks later. "I tink dis might be de break ve are looking for." She sounded excited. Her body was exhausted by the amount of work a servant was expected to do.

"I've registered with the temp agency Anya told you they use. Maybe I'll get hired," Alice responded. She'd planned for this eventuality. They didn't know how many people on their list would be there, but from what she had gotten from those computers, they had a lot on about two dozen possibles. The list could grow from the spiderwebbing they had found.

"Stay avay from Mr. Bogomolov," Sasha advised. "He tinks he is a ladykiller. Charming, but he doesn't realize dey all despise him." She went on to tell her that he had already raped the nanny. Anya had pleaded with her new friend not to say anything and Willow had promised.

Alice didn't like what she was hearing. It was her experience that someone who arrogantly got away with what people like this did,

continued on in such a fashion. They felt they couldn't be touched, they couldn't be harmed. They were wrong. Alice was willing to teach them.

~ ~ ~ ~ ~

Alice was pleased to get a call on her new cell. She and Sasha had both gotten cell phones on a Russian network while they were in Russia. They kept the others hidden along with the laptop in the floorboards that Alice had pried up from their sublet. They had a one-night job for her at the home of Mr. and Mrs. Bogomolov…was she interested? They named a sum that was exceedingly low and Alice was insulted for anyone who worked at such wages, but she pretended to be thrilled at the prospect of work and accepted. She went for a uniform the next day.

The home was impressive, but then Alice knew that from Sasha's descriptions. It had the French provincial influence and all the wood was lined in gold leaf. At some point it had all been restored and it looked charming, just not to Alice's taste. She was shown to the servants' quarters, introduced to everyone including Willow, and told that she should help cook. After all, that and sex were all a woman was good for, right? She nearly hit the housekeeper who told her that, shocked that a woman would believe such baloney much less say it.

Alice listened to the cook's complaints and followed her directions efficiently. She helped Willow and the other maid to serve the various courses and it was then that she got an idea. She recognized several of the people dining there that evening, not only from the dossiers she was compiling with Sasha, but from the keylogger program that she had followed to other computers. She'd managed to obtain a disk that automatically translated the odd symbols of the Russian alphabet into

English. It wasn't perfect and the grammar was frequently off, but it was enough that Alice was in the computers of at least six people now, several of whom were here at the dinner. She could feel something rise within her. These people had ordered her and Sasha's imprisonment without a second thought. While she would love to do the same to them, she knew that it wouldn't be possible. She wouldn't engage the resources. Instead, her revenge would be subtle and painful.

While the cook worked on another course, Alice deboned the fish that would be in their dinner that evening. She quickly looked for and found an empty jar and put the bones she plucked from the spine of the fish inside along with some alcohol.

"Vhat are you doing?" Sasha, as Willow, asked, aghast as she watched Alice.

"I'm pickling them," Alice said succinctly and looked around to see if she was being observed as she finished. She quickly hid the jar behind the stove to warm it so it would quickly do what she needed. She wasn't sure when she would have the opportunity, but she would use what she had on hand as she continued to work diligently.

"Ah, you are good helper," the Russian cook slapped Alice on the back, nearly unseating her from where she was cutting up vegetables.

Alice smiled. She had understood the woman from listening to her CDs and from talking in town, but she didn't respond. She kept up with her work, letting that speak for her. She enjoyed the feel of the knife in her hand as she cut rapidly and effectively.

"Most of these people are spending the night. The Popovs live here in town," Willow mentioned as she went by to collect another dish to serve.

Alice filed that away. She was only engaged for the night and it would take at least until the following day for the fish bones to pickle properly. She had to make herself indispensable somehow.

She watched as the other senior maid snuck candies and chocolates when the cook wasn't looking. It gave her an idea.

"May I use the bathroom?" she asked the cook respectfully in her halting Russian.

The woman smiled and agreed, directing the French woman to the bathroom that all the servants used.

Alice went directly to the medicine cabinet after locking the door and peeing. After all, she might be on her feet the rest of the night and not get another chance, she might as well take it while she could. Inside the medicine cabinet was a jumble of castoff pills, packages, and an overall mess. Alice didn't read the packages, she couldn't with their strange Russian script, but she did recognize a name. Smiling, she quickly popped an entire sheet of them into her apron. Moving the mess about in the cabinet so no one would know they were missing, and then washing her hands, she headed back to her work station.

In the next half-hour she managed to pop all the small chocolate nuggets out of the medicine pack and place them in the pantry from where the senior maid was taking her stolen breaks. Alice gleefully anticipated the woman finding them and wasn't disappointed when she saw her start eating them. She put extra there so the woman would think they were plentiful. By the end of the long, drawn-out dinner with its many courses, the maid was in agony, sick as could be. A foul stench followed her from the bathroom where she ended up many times, the laxative making quick work of her body's functions.

"You go home," the cook ordered angrily as she sniffed suspiciously. She was angry and disgusted by the odor on her maid.

"I don't know what happened or what I ate..." she began apologetically. Alice didn't look up from the dishes she was now scrubbing; they were too large for the dishwasher.

"You!" the cook rounded on Alice, who looked up, alarmed. "Can you work tomorrow?"

Alice nodded and tried to look grateful at the possibility of more work.

The cook had her arriving at 5am, after working so late at this dinner. Alice knew she would be dragging, but she couldn't pass up the opportunity to serve those people a meal...one they would never remember or forget.

As she finished cleaning up the kitchen, she unobtrusively slipped the last of the chocolate laxatives in her pocket along with the package they had come in. As she looked around the now clean kitchen she smiled evilly in anticipation of the next morning's meal.

"You, you will serve," the cook ordered both Alice and Sasha. They exchanged looks. Both had arrived on time the next morning to hear that the senior maid had been unable to work, she was quite ill and no one knew why. They both knew, as Alice had thrown away the package on the way home and flushed the laxatives once inside their sublet. Before they left the sublet, Alice had started a program on their computer; it would mine the information from the six computers that she had targeted. All six people were at the Bogomolov home as guests.

Alice waited until the cook was distracted by dishing up the oatmeal for the first part of their guest's breakfast. She took out her jar and pulled the now pickled fish bones from the alcohol. She curled them into small shapes, too small to detect, twirling them into tiny circles, and while the cook dished up more onto another tray she dropped several fish bones on top of the dishes that Sasha was holding. Onto that she sprinkled

cinnamon and placed thin sliced peaches and strawberries to make it look appetizing. She took the next tray in without the fish bones.

While Sasha served her tray to select people, Alice served hers to the others. This way only the specific people they were targeting would get the dishes of fish-boned oatmeal.

"But what if they don't like oatmeal?" Sasha had fretted.

"Enough of them will eat it that it should work," Alice promised.

Alice was just surprised that the guests were all up for this early morning breakfast, but apparently they had a meeting later and the Bogomolovs were hosting. She was only sorry that they wouldn't be able to give the Popolovs some of the oatmeal. She would have to think up something else for them.

Alice helped serve the courses of breakfast, surprised and delighted by how many ate the oatmeal that had been served. She was actually pleased to gather the empty dishes and take them back to the kitchen to serve another course. She helped clean up the kitchen and went on her way, released for the day. They wouldn't need extra help anymore.

"Vhat have you done?" Sasha asked when she returned from work later that day.

"Those bones will eventually return back to shape and become skewers in their intestines. It's a very painful way for them to die, don't you think?" Alice smiled and her cat-like eyes were yellow.

Sasha stared in horror as she realized what Alice had done.

"We've also got seed money," she pointed at the computer screen where her program had finished hours ago. Alice now had access to the fortunes of the six people they had targeted. "Do you know if any of these people are in the hospital yet?" she asked

"Both of the Bogomolovs left the house late this afternoon; they were very sick with cramps," Sasha told her, wondering how anyone knew how to do these things.

"Good, I think it's time that we drain their accounts," Alice said succinctly and began transferring sums out of the accounts. She did the same for four others, but not the Popovs as they hadn't eaten at the breakfast. By that evening, Alice had set up dummy accounts to put the money into, linking them to The Assemblage through 'similar', but false names, ones that would momentarily be recognized by anyone trying to find the trail of money before it disappeared into real accounts that Alice held.

"You share dat with me, right?" Sasha asked as she realized the amounts of money they were talking about.

"You hold a ruble up next to another ruble and you tell me which one is yours and which one is mine?" Alice asked her.

Sasha looked at Alice in consternation before the sense of what she was saying began to penetrate. "Okay," she answered. "Fifty-fifty."

Alice smiled now that she had made her point and then shook her head. "We shall see, my friend, we shall see."

Sasha wasn't so sure it would be fifty-fifty, but she had to trust Alice. From what she understood, Alice had just dealt a major blow to The Assemblage. Alice explained how the program worked and how the money was filtered through the various accounts until it 'disappeared.' She was amazed at this woman's knowledge and only glad she was on her side and not her enemy's.

The newspaper screamed that several people attending a party at the Bogomolovs including the Bogomolovs themselves, had been poisoned. As Sasha read the paper to Alice, they both shook their heads knowing that the people hadn't been poisoned at all. Only an autopsy would reveal the

true cause of death. Some Russians would not permit such a thing of their loved ones, a violation of their bodies, and as a result they would never know the true cause of death. Alice had counted on this.

"We must go to these funerals," she told Sasha.

"How? Vhy? I've been laid off and I didn't vork for the Bogomolovs long enough that I should attend…?"

"We have to find a way to attend," Alice mused. It was too perfect an opportunity to find some of the others on their list. One of those they had managed to kill had been in attendance at the beating of Lexi and for that alone Sasha was pleased with the results. She was horrified at how painful it must have been for those people, but a perforated intestine was a fine way for those pigs to die.

~ ~ ~ ~ ~

Alice knew that boys were boys the world over. She used bribery to get herself in as a replacement for one of the boys helping with the church service for the Bogomolovs. She knew that some of The Assemblage would attend, but even she was surprised at the number that did. Even those they only suspected of being a part of Sasha's imprisonment were there. Sasha was sitting up in the balcony and hissing into a microphone that was deeply implanted in the 'boy's' ear. Alice sent her dirty looks from time to time to quiet her enthusiasm as she pointed out people to her.

The priest looked at the boy oddly. 'He' didn't look quite like a boy. He was thin like the teens they used in their service, and small, but he couldn't quite remember this particular pretty boy's face. He really must retire next year. He couldn't even remember all the words of the service. As Alice held the golden tray of wafers that were to represent the body of

Christ, a sleight of hand had her handing the priest a special wafer she prepared for certain people. Since the tray was full of them, she must use this sleight of hand unobtrusively.

Looking up at Sasha to confirm those they have tagged for this communion, she verifies that she has the right people. Although she recognizes several, she is pleased most by Popov, one of the hierarchies of The Assemblage, when he comes forward for the ceremony. He looks at the boy oddly, wondering why he looks familiar, but not realizing it is Alice he is seeing. He doesn't recognize her from the pictures he has seen of Sasha Brenhov and Alice Weaver together in New York and he doesn't recognize her as the maid in the Bogomolov's home. Instead he is left with a vague feeling that he knows that boy from 'somewhere.' He takes the wafer offered to him by the priest, washing it down with the blood of Christ in the form of wine.

~ ~ ~ ~ ~

Alice was pleased. Two more of the web had been identified and she had followed them from the church. Sasha had seen the 'come along' signal and followed Alice towards an obtrusive black sedan that was now parked outside a bar. She watched as Alice slid underneath the vehicle, fiddled with something, and then slipped out just as quickly. She then saw Alice cut a small triangle from a back window, wondering why she did so.

"Vhat have you done?" she asked as they hurried away.

"I put a clip on the fuel line. It will make the car run out of gas quickly," she told her as they went to another bar to get a meal.

"Vhat vill dat do?"

"It will allow us to catch those two guys who hit Lexi," Alice told her.

"Dose ver dem?" she asked, angrily and Alice caught her arm when she would have gone back.

Alice nodded, having recognized them in the church. They weren't really part of The Assemblage, merely hirelings. The death of one of The Assemblage involved in Lexi's beating was only part of it. "I'll go back later, they will be there a while," she said, pointing with her thumb back at the other bar. She'd heard it was a particular meeting place for some people. They would be there for quite a while if she didn't miss her guess.

"Vhy the vindow?"

Alice just smiled as she replied, "You'll see."

Alice was annoyed with how much time it took her quarry to finish at the bar. The men were hearty in their appreciation of their fallen comrade. They came out of the bar weaving. Her disgust at the fact that they had beaten a woman, a helpless woman, Lexi, turned to even more anger over the fact that they were going to drink and drive. She rubbed her arms at the cold she was experiencing as she waited for the fools.

"Vhy don't you turn on your lights," Sasha asked, naively after they had two close calls when other cars nearly hit them in the dark.

"We don't want them," she indicated the now weaving car in front of them, "to notice us following them." She was pleased to see they were heading out of town.

Sasha realized she should have figured that out. She was cold, tired, and the day had been fraught with a lot of emotion as they attended the funeral. Alice had assured her that the people she slipped the wafers to would be dead this night. She also told her that they would have to move on shortly. While she was sure they wouldn't be suspected, she was also sure this many of The Assemblage killed in such a short span of time

would alert the others and send them into hiding. It was time to go hunting them, one at a time, in their own homes.

Alice was slowing the car, well back from the other car that had pulled over to the side of the road. Under the street light, the two women could just make out that the men were drunkenly inspecting their car. Alice wondered if they would discover her clip, but was certain it was unlikely in their inebriated state. She saw them both indicate the evening was too cold to be out by slapping their arms and stomping their feet. She was pleased to see them sit inside the car at the side of the road as they discussed their situation.

"Come on," she breathed to Sasha, reaching in the back seat for a bag.

"Vhat, vhat has happened?" Sasha asked, wonderingly. She looked to see what Alice had seen that was different from what she herself had observed.

Alice was now pleased to realize these two were very drunk, probably their last glasses of alcohol had fully kicked in now. While the car wasn't really out of gas, it was slow to release it from the clip squeezing their fuel line. She looked up as she approached the car...it was starting to snow. They tried to drive it forward again and didn't see her approach. It conked out half a block away where it was really dark away from the street light. Alice couldn't be more pleased as she smiled to herself. She heard them swearing at their predicament.

"Vhat are ve doing?" Sasha whispered, knowing their voices would carry in the dark. She glanced at the falling snow, wondering how bad the winter would be here and *knowing* it would be bad because it was Russia and far north. It was early in the season for this, but that didn't mean anything.

Alice didn't answer her. Carefully, because she didn't want to be observed in the car's rearview mirrors, she pulled out a tube and began to

squeeze it into the edges of the door. The two men inside the car were having an argument and were totally distracted. She handed the bag to Sasha and whispered, "Put one end over the exhaust pipe while I glue the other door." Sasha looked at her, startled. She had no idea what they were about to do.

Sasha opened the bag and found a rubber hose with an odd end to it. It was larger than the actual hose, but she found it fit over the exhaust pipe. She attached it carefully, as the pipe was hot. She could feel the heat momentarily through her gloves as she fitted the hose over the exhaust pipe.

Alice quickly squirted the epoxy into the doorframe, hoping, as it stated, that it would not freeze in the cold air. She stayed below the window line and thanked the powers-that-be that the two were arguing and not paying attention. She turned back to help Sasha, knowing the other woman was confused by these goings-on since Alice hadn't really explained herself. She found her looking at the hose, holding it away from herself as the fumes were spilling out of the tube from the barely running car. "Here," she breathed, holding out a hand for it, which Sasha willingly handed her.

Sasha watched as Alice went to the side of the car where she had cut out the little triangle of glass. She squeezed her tube of glue around the edges of the glass as well as on the rubber hose that was spewing its toxins. She inserted the hose, held it for a while, and then quickly went under the car looking for the clip. It was very dark and she reached in her pocket for her penlight. The car was hot, and she could feel the heat from the engine as she looked for and found the fuel line. She released the clip, sending more gas that the car desperately needed into the occasionally

sputtering engine. She quickly got out from under the running car and stood up next to Sasha.

"Let's go," she breathed quietly to Sasha as she pulled her along.

"But vhat?" Sasha began automatically, but knew this wasn't the time or the place to ask questions. If Alice answered them at all, it would be better when they were in their small apartment. She hurried to keep up with the smaller woman, carrying the bag. They got in their own car, which started easily. She was grateful for the fact that Alice had gotten rid of that Yugo so long ago. This car warmed up quickly when she started it, heat pouring from the vents. "Now vhat?" she murmured as they looked at the car in front of them. She wasn't expecting a response.

"Do you want to watch or go back to the apartment?" Alice asked as she peered through the night at the car in front of them. She smiled as she saw it begin to drive away, she knew that the emissions would be pouring into the car and poisoning the two henchmen.

"Let's go," Sasha said distastefully. She was trying to figure out if Alice enjoyed what she had been doing or if it was just a necessary task. They had killed many people over the past few days and it hadn't seemed to affect the petite woman either way.

Alice turned their car around, turning on the lights once again and watching in her rearview mirror as the taillights of the car in back of them drove away until she couldn't see them anymore. She knew the snow would soon cover any tracks they may have made and the car would soon be far away from the crime scene. She drove carefully back to their apartment.

Pulling off her winter clothes—a necessary evil, as it got colder by the day—Alice hung them up in the apartment.

"Are you hungry?" Sasha asked as she headed to their small refrigerator to look and to stop thinking about the day.

"No, I have work to do," Alice responded and pulled the laptop from its hidden place. She fired it up and quickly got online looking for emails that her programs would automatically send her. She found two of particular interest. Apparently the wafers had been successful and their spouses were already checking out their banking accounts and other financial information. With the worm she had planted, a kind of keylogger information program, she now had access to these people's records. She started up another program, slowly draining these people's bank accounts. Whoever had accessed them would find that their rubles, euros, and other ill-gotten money would be gone by morning.

Alice had set up a network of phony companies. Using the internet, she had 'hired' people to 'purchase' property and companies that the Brenhovs had previously owned as well as other properties she could divest them of for hard currency. After these 'purchases', the former owner would find their bank accounts empty of any monies they had received. If they gave Alice's employees their accounts, it was just a matter of time before she accessed them. If they transferred the funds to a foreign account, Alice's keylogger programs would find not only the accounts, but the passwords as well, and she could take that money too. It was terribly time-consuming, but Alice was efficient in her desire to bankrupt these people.

Alice planted funds in the two thugs' accounts that would lead The Assemblage to believe they were in on some of the killings and divert attention away from Alice and Sasha. While she knew they were being looked for, no one knew where they were at the moment. They didn't need to know that Alice was killing them, or to what extent she was involved.

Sasha watched as Alice tapped away at the laptop. She was relieved that anytime she wanted to look on it, it was there with their agreed upon

passwords to share. She understood the financials when Alice showed them to her, but she couldn't grasp the concept of the programs that the woman was using. All she saw was that they were eliminating men and women from The Assemblage and it was this organization that was responsible for their imprisonment.

~ ~ ~ ~ ~

"Look here," Alice pointed out a sign she recognized. While she didn't read the Russian script, she knew a 'for rent' sign when she saw one.

They were looking for a place to stay since they had given up their apartment in Vologda. They were near a small village in central Russia after they had taken a train out of town, storing their car against further use. Alice had found that one of their prey, the Filipov family, had escaped to their country estate. The emails she had gleaned showed agitation in The Assemblage ranks.

As The Assemblage shared the spoils of their business dealings, the fact that the monies were disappearing was causing this agitation. The families that had thought themselves solvent against anything, were now destitute and seeking out others of The Assemblage, but they wanted nothing to do with the heirs of the deceased. Some felt it was not their problem. Some felt they were cursed. Others were speculating at the fact that only certain members of The Assemblage had been targeted. The deaths had been horrible. Look at the Bogomolovs who died in terrible pain. Their guests had been carefully chosen and the survivors were now suspect. Finding the two henchmen dead in a ditch, their car doors glued shut, the hose from the tailpipe clearly indicating how they had been killed, rattled a few people. This spoke of mob killings and while The Assemblage was above the Russian mob, a few of its members had been

active in it not so long ago. They recognized the signs. Who was targeting these members of The Assemblage?

"Ve should look," Sasha told her.

"Speak Russian, it's the only way I'm going to learn," Alice said, exasperated. She had a hard time learning the language. Even after all the months she had been listening to the CDs and interacting with the people, it was still a hard language to learn.

Sasha grinned. She had seen her friend's frustration, but Russian, like English, had many dialects and phrases that couldn't be translated. It was amusing as the American woman usually picked up so many things easily with her brilliant mind, but this was not so easy.

They called the number on the sign and Alice was pleased that the landlord lived a few doors away and would show them the place immediately.

"You have work?" he asked, succinctly. No one came to this small village to live without a job.

Alice nodded and in careful Russian answered, "Yes, I work online. I'm grateful that I don't need to go out to work." For effect she had been wearing a scarf that she pulled across her face slightly to hide her features as though ashamed of them. The man bought her reasoning although he could tell Russian wasn't her first language.

"We don't have internet here," he told her, almost proud of that fact.

"I was told it would come into the village this spring. I can commute," she answered, almost sad at the fact that she would have to go out. She pulled her scarf against her face again.

He nodded. He had heard that too, but then things moved slowly in this area. "What about you?" he asked the other woman looking at Sasha.

"She supports both of us, but I will look for work," she said proudly, knowing that belligerence would be effective when dealing with this man. She was right. He admired her proud spirit and the fact that she would willingly work.

Alice knew that cash would make the man more willing to rent to them. The apartment, while small, would suit them. Best of all it was furnished, something they hadn't found in other apartments they had looked at. She didn't want to shop for furniture, but she needed her comforts. The only thing that alarmed her was that this village was so small and they wouldn't have access to the internet. They would have to find public internet in a larger village or city and, without a car, they were at a disadvantage. She was willing to take that disadvantage for the time being to get at this particular woman who was part of The Assemblage and hiding on her estate. It would also make them less noticeable. Who would expect to find the two women they were looking for in this small village so close to their prey?

They rented the apartment month-to-month although the man wanted a lease. Alice explained her job might take her out of town because of the fact they had no internet. She would pay monthly in cash, if that was all right with him?

Cash had a tendency to make people do foolish things. He rented to them without a contract, handing over the keys without a qualm. "Don't break anything," he warned them and pointed out the market where they could stock their small cupboard.

"Do you think we can find the Filipov estate?" Sasha asked as soon as they were alone. They had put their luggage down and begun to unpack. Alice's luggage mainly consisted of gadgets and things she knew they might need to go after their quarry.

"Shhhh, we don't want anyone to know we are looking for it. We have to get to know the locals. Be seen. Start to fit in and perhaps overhear something," she advised.

"That can take months," she pointed out.

"Are you in a hurry to scare them off?"

Sasha sighed. She knew Alice was right. They were hunting these people. After the initial group was gone, they had done exactly what Alice had foreseen…they were hiding. It would take time to root them out. She was determined though. The more they found out about these people, the more she realized they had targeted not only herself, but many other people. Eliminating these people from the earth was not a bad penalty for them. The fact that they had ordered her kidnapping was the least of the things they had done. The Filipov woman they were now pursuing was involved in high stakes gambling and prostitution. That a woman would do this to other women disgusted Sasha.

Alice managed to get them both jobs in a local pub. She had cajoled the owner, telling him she was still learning Russian, an obvious truth evidenced by her speaking of the language, and told him she wanted only part-time because of her internet job. She had to take the train out of the village in order to go to the next city and use public internet to catch up on the emails and delve further into the financials on the web that she was slowly accumulating information on. The amounts of money she had already moved were staggering, but didn't pay for the time she was away from her family. As she explained to Sasha, it would never pay in money, only lives.

Two pretty women, both with different shades of red hair—Alice had decided they would change it to black in their next town—one with short spikes, the other with long tresses, attracted some attention at the bar.

For the first time in her life, Alice found that being a waitress sucked. The men groped and treated her badly, the tips were awful for the amount of time she was on her feet delivering drinks and putting up with their behavior, and women were haughty to the pretty woman.

Sasha, attempting to bartend, wasn't faring much better, but at least she understood the language clearly. It was she that heard of the Filipov estate before Alice could.

"They are east of here," she explained from what she had learned.

"That's vague," Alice said tiredly, rubbing her sore feet from a day's work. She was just glad it was part-time. She was killing herself and her strength wasn't what it used to be. She had more respect for waiters and waitresses after this gig.

Sasha laughed, used to Alice's wry sense of humor. "I heard they might entertain one weekend," she said with a smile.

Alice perked up at this. That might mean other members of The Assemblage attending, maybe an opportunity to eliminate more of these people. The amount of time it was taking was depressing her as they wintered in Russia.

"With the Christmas holidays coming up, they are known to throw a party," she confided.

Alice nodded. This could work out in their favor. Now she would have to find out anything and everything about the party. She was off the next day and had a train ticket to another city. She had to check their internet information and keep up the premise that she had a job online. The sporadic pillaging of their accounts had now slowed to a trickle due to her inability to get online all the time. Alice actually thought this was a bonus since it meant they were less noticeable.

"They will have to come through the village on the train if they don't drive," she pointed out.

Sasha nodded. She had thought of that. "Maybe they will hire from the village?"

Alice nodded in agreement, but didn't count on that. Since they had hired on to get the Bogomolovs and their guests, they certainly couldn't think that ruse would work twice. She was wrong.

"Hey there, honey. Would you like to go back to my place?" an arm around her waist ensured that Alice was unable to deliver the rest of her drinks on her tray. She balanced them carefully as the man felt up her waist.

"How would you like me to hurt you?" she asked, philosophically.

"Oooh, with heels and maybe fishnet stockings?" he cooed, disgusting her.

Alice smiled. She was wearing jeans, casual shoes, and a nondescript shirt. She fit in with the other villagers…just someone trying to make a living. Nothing about what she wore or did should be attracting attention.

Just the fact that Alice and Sasha were new in the village made them targets. Alice, with her short spikey hair, stood out. They thought perhaps she was part of the punk phase, but just a bit too old for that group. Sasha, appearing a little more refined and obviously never having bartended before, was thought to be down on her luck. Alice had inwardly laughed, wondering what they would think if these people ever realized they were in the presence of a billionairess who normally had people make drinks *for* her.

"Look, you're going to get me fired," she told him pointedly, glancing at the manager who was looking at her angrily. He'd already warned Sasha to stop mixing the wrong drinks or she would go, although Alice doubted that, as hard as it was to find people to work in this small village.

"Maybe I could interest you in a position?" he asked with as much insinuation as possible.

"No, thanks."

"C'mon, give me a try," he pleaded, using his other hand to feel up her thigh.

Alice was ready to knock him in the head with the tray containing the drinks. "Let me go," she warned him instead.

"C'mon baby, don't you know who I am?"

Alice chose to grab one of the drinks she knew contained whiskey. It would hurt, she knew, when it splashed in his eyes. He let her go immediately. "Who is that?" she asked the manager as she went to pay for the drink she had 'spilled' and get a replacement.

"That is Mr. Fillipov. He and his wife live out on a farm east of here," he told her with a laugh. She had handled herself well despite the man's groping, and she didn't bitch about paying for the drink.

Alice perked up at that news, but then knew that having spilled a drink, rather having splashed it in the man's face, wasn't likely to endear her to him. She was wrong. She hated to be wrong normally, but in this case she was pleased.

"Look, I'm sorry about before, but the job offer still stands," he told her later when he had a chance. He was holding up his hands showing he wasn't going to touch her.

"What kind of a job?" she asked, suspiciously.

"My wife and I throw parties from time to time. We could use some extra servers," he told her diplomatically. He was eyeing her like he still wanted to see her in those fishnet stockings.

Alice hesitated. It would be the perfect opportunity to size up the estate. She hadn't lied to Sasha when she said that they might meet others of The Assemblage there. Her hesitation worked in her favor.

He mentioned a payment that she was quite surprised to hear. Used to slave wages, she immediately accepted and then asked, "What about my friend?" Her head took in the inadequate bartender that Sasha was.

"Well…" he hesitated now.

"She could serve too," Alice quickly added, knowing Sasha sucked as a bartender unless it was straight shots or beer from the bottle—even beer on tap she managed to screw up with too much froth and not enough beer.

The man smiled. Two pretty women at their party couldn't be a bad thing. "I'll let you know when and how to get there," he promised and slipped her a tip. Unfortunately, he chose to slip it into the small amount of cleavage Alice was showing and she slapped his hand, nearly dropping the bill. "Easy," he admonished, but smiled charmingly as he left the bar.

Alice took the money, but she wasn't as thrilled with the offer. The man was a letch. She wondered what kind of parties he and his wife had out at their farm…she had thought it an estate. Since his wife was into prostitution she could only surmise they were sex parties. Knowing many women and men were held almost captive by this industry, she didn't have any respect for these people.

"Have you heard from him?" Sasha asked nearly a week later. She'd been thrilled that Alice got the job offer and managed to finagle one for her. She was anxious to move on from this hunt. The apartment was cold most of the time and she hated working as a bartender. She knew she was bad at it, and while she was learning, she was too slow for most of the patrons. She hated being bad at anything.

"Nope, not a word. We may have to crash their party," she explained with a grimace. She had been right, from what she overheard, they were sex parties. The women trucked in en masse for the Filipov's friends who were promised a weekend of debauchery.

Alice wasn't asked to work it again, but Sasha was invited as a guest. This alone made them both suspicious when the invitation came to the bar.

"Should I accept? Should I go?" Sasha asked Alice worriedly. She was almost excited that she had been asked.

"Let me think," Alice mulled it over. It was possible that Sasha had been recognized. Alice had carefully worn makeup that made it look like she had a scar and allowed her to hide her face with the scarf. In the bar though, the scar merely marred the pretty face of the woman. Filipov had groped and invited her to work anyway, despite her appearance. She wondered why they hadn't been contacted again and why the invitation. It could be a trap. The more she thought about it, the more she thought it was a trap. Somehow, they had been made. As she explained her thoughts, something she was not used to doing for anyone, but had learned to do for Sasha's sake, she thought about what they would do.

"I think you should decline." She finished with, "Maybe we should move on."

"And let those thieves go?" Sasha asked, outraged. She was determined to get every single one of these people who had so callously ordered her imprisonment and stolen from her! Not only for the lost time, but also the emotions, the money, and the things they had done to her beloved Lexi.

"No, they will pay, but I have to think this out," she promised.

Sasha did end up declining the invitation. Neither of the women knew how much this displeased the Filipovs. Alice had discovered that the Filipovs were not pure Russian, but were of Bulgarian extract, living in Russia and pillaging money where they could, living off of prostitutes and other illegal activities.

A few days later, Alice had just returned from the city and a very productive day on the internet. She'd gotten a lot of information on some

of the members they had yet to find. The two pictures that hadn't been filled in were two of the Baltizar brothers, they thought. One of them was the man she had overheard in the library so long ago. Sasha had identified him only as an albino; the whole family were albinos. Alice knew that albinism was a genetic disorder. It stopped the melanocyte cells from producing enough melanin. Melanin gives the skin pigmentation and protects the cells from being damaged by the sun. From what Alice had gleaned on the Baltizars so far, at least two of the brothers and the father were all albinos. The two brothers were definitely part of The Assemblage, but Alice hadn't yet found definitive proof of any involvement by the rest of the family.

As Alice walked from the train station to their small, dingy, and rarely heated apartment, she saw a well-to-do car pull up in front of the place. She watched as a woman got out with a man and assessed the building before heading towards their apartment. With a well-aimed shot from some type of gun, they broke a small window and she could see a canister projected into the apartment. The two ran back to their car and drove away rapidly. Alice ran the rest of the way to the apartment, unlocked the door, and left it wide to air out the apartment. She began to look desperately for Sasha as she held her breath. She heard the shower going. Sasha hadn't even heard the breaking of the glass as whatever was in that canister filled their apartment. Alice went back outside into the cold and took several deep breaths. Her eyes had watered, but she was sure whatever was in the apartment was meant for their lungs. She went back inside and began opening windows, most of which were frozen shut. She ran back outside, feeling light-headed from holding her breath. She returned after several deep breaths in the cold, crisp air. Then she heard the shower turn off and knew she had to return.

Sasha was startled as she came out of the small bathroom to find Alice in front of her. Alice grabbed her, held her nose, and put her own mouth over Sasha's. In all the time they had been together, neither had made a pass at the other. This unexpected assault jarred the Russian woman. She missed Lexi, her girlfriend and lover, more than she could imagine, but she would never cheat on her. She knew Alice felt the same about Kathy. What was this?

Alice held tightly to the struggling woman. Sasha was larger than the petite Alice, but Alice held on like a monkey. With her fingers pinching Sasha's nose shut tightly, Alice maneuvered the woman out the open door and outside before she let go and pulled back, letting them both pull clean air into their oxygen-starved lungs.

"What was that?" Sasha demanded when she was able to speak once again. She was heaving from the effort and she could faintly smell something in the air.

"Someone...shot...something...through...our...windows," Alice gasped as she leaned over to draw lungsful of air into herself.

"They did what?" she looked around as though she could see the perpetrators.

Alice held up a hand as she got her breath back. Slowly she stood up again and explained what she had seen. "They obviously know who we are or at least suspect."

Sasha was shocked. They had perpetrated some truly horrendous crimes, but no one had caught them, not yet. The thought of going back to a prison or being held captive truly frightened her. It also angered her. "What can we do?" she asked, angrily.

Despite the fact that they spoke almost exclusively in Russian now for the benefit of Alice, they were both aware that they could be overheard. There were other tenants after all. Alice held up a hand. Taking in a deep

breath she went back into the apartment. Her eyes didn't water as much as she turned on the overhead fan. She went back outside where Sasha stood shivering in the cold, grabbing the other woman's coat on her way. "Here. Let's let that air out a while more," she said.

Alice and Sasha stood on their doorstep a long time, waiting for the gasses to dissipate. Only after Alice checked once more did they go in and find the canister. It was clearly marked poison, right down to the skull and crossbones.

"Start packing," Alice advised. Whether these people knew who Alice and Sasha really were or not, they had to go.

"Where will we go?"

"Just pack," Alice ordered, quickly pulling their laptop and other things from the floorboards. As she stuffed things in the bags they had brought, she was pleased to see the nail gun. She was even more pleased that she had kept the main battery pack and the extra one fully charged. She had a feeling she would need them, and soon.

~ ~ ~ ~ ~

Alice knew that whether the Filipovs knew who they really were or not, they were most likely behind the attack on them in their apartment. She had made sure to take the canister that had been projected into their apartment. They had posted a handwritten letter to their landlord telling him that the lack of heat in the apartment (now compounded by the hole in the window) was the reason they were moving out. They simply left.

Alice had a general idea now where the Filipovs lived and they headed east. It was really too cold to walk, but they had no choice. Carrying their bags, they looked like vagabonds. When they saw a farm in the distance,

they quickly entered the barn for warmth, curling up together to try to stop their shivering.

"This is ridiculous! I have the money to stay at the Ritz," Sasha bitched as she tucked her hands under her arms.

"Don't you know? This IS the Ritz," Alice joked. "Country style Ritz," she joked, making a double entendre reference to Ritz crackers versus the Ritz Hotel. She hoped Sasha got it.

She didn't, but she understood that the barn could be considered a hotel and thought it was amusing. "I'm going to be hungry in the morning."

"I pulled the dry goods we had," Alice informed her and reached for a bag. The small penlight they were using showed her opening a zippered duffel.

"Do you think we will freeze to death?" Sasha asked, fearfully.

"I'm more afraid if this farmer has a dog," Alice answered as she handed over some thin bread and cheese.

The two of them ate and kept their thoughts to themselves. It was cold, but not as cold as the dead of winter would be. This was only the beginning of winter in Russia.

"If you could be anywhere in the world right now, where would you be?" Sasha began. They had played this game many times over the year they had been together.

"That's easy…" Alice began, but was interrupted by Sasha.

"And Palos Verdes is off the map."

Alice grinned. "I'd like to be back on my island with Kathy. The kids would be safe and asleep and it would just be her and I on the beach."

"A beach sounds nice right now," Sasha agreed and they both continued to think about all the places they had ever visited. They had shared many stories like this.

After eating, they both dozed off, but Alice was glad when the call of nature woke her and she had to go pee. She wasn't certain it wasn't cold enough to freeze to death, but she knew falling asleep in such cold would kill them if it was. The exercise it took to climb down the ladder and find a place to pee, then to poop and find something to clean herself with, was enough to wake her up. She went back into the hayloft to wake Sasha. She was sure the exercise would do the woman good.

The next day they were up, but only after the farmer left his barn after doing his chores. He apparently didn't have a farm dog and for that they were grateful. He did, however, have cats…lots of cats. Alice had woken to five of them watching the two women sleep. She hadn't noticed them when they had gone into the barn, but obviously the animals knew they were there. She was amused and held out her hand, a more adventurous one came forward to smell it and be petted. She soon found herself trying to pet three cats at the same time, the other two looking suspiciously at the strange woman. Sasha woke from her warm cocoon in the hay to find Alice fending off their exuberant advances and chuckling.

"I did not know you liked cats," she stated with a smile.

"I like all animals," Alice confided. "Years ago, I got a dog for the kids, a golden retriever. I miss her. She was so much fun on walks, very playful."

~ ~ ~ ~ ~

Alice could not know that her dog had been killed and as Kathy related this to her, interrupting her recitation of her story, she was saddened at the news. She had known the dog was gone, but hearing Kathy tell her the details, how she had actually felt, angered Alice. She was glad she had

taken out those responsible, but she hadn't gotten to that part in her story and she verbally returned to Russia as she told Kathy the reasons she was gone for so long.

~ ~ ~ ~ ~

They found the large farm that constituted the Filipov family estate. Alice was pleased to find she wasn't that far off from what she gleaned previously. They would have found it the previous day, but it wasn't directly east as she had been told. They walked through woods and grasslands until they came to the farm. They were fortunate that they hadn't gotten lost, but they were in sight of the road that led them there. It was a surprise to find out it was a pig farm, that is until they observed Galina Filipov feeding some*one* to the pigs. Alice and Sasha had taken up residence in the hayloft of this barn too and were on hand to witness the woman murder someone. The squeals of the pigs were horrendous. They were boars really, with tusks and a dirty complexion. The woman seemed to get some sort of sexual satisfaction out of it from what Alice observed. Galina really enjoyed watching the pigs first kill, and then eat, the human victim.

They didn't know what the person had done, but Alice was really disgusted as she watched it. Sasha pulled back slowly in the hayloft and vomited into a corner. She didn't return to watch the animals eat the human remains.

"They must die," Sasha ascertained firmly later, "all of them."

Alice couldn't agree more. The pigs had left nothing that could implicate the Filipovs in the death of the man that Galina had fed them. She wondered how many times they had used this particular method of killing.

"We should poison them," Sasha stated.

"Why would I use poison? Torture is so much more…satisfying."

Sasha wasn't sure Alice was teasing…looking at the glint in her odd yellow-orange eyes, she thought she was serious.

They stayed out in the barn, hiding from any of the workers that came around to muck out the pig stalls. There were cattle too, but these were kept out in the field except for those that were milked. The workers didn't stay too long and hurried away from their work as soon as they could. They had homes on the farm. Alice used the dark of night to scope out the Kozlov's farmhouse.

It really wasn't that small of a farmhouse. It was designed for entertaining…large rooms with nice furnishings abounded from what Alice could see through the windows with her night vision goggles. No one patrolled the place so Alice was sure they thought themselves safe out here in the middle of nowhere. She was more certain of that fact as she climbed to the second story of the large house and found women and men in various stages of dress—an orgy was going on. She recognized Galina Filipov in a dominatrix costume. Her husband was on his hands and knees in leathers, being humiliated and enjoying every moment of it.

Alice liked a healthy sex life. She and Kathy had enjoyed themselves, had used toys from time to time, but they had always respected each other and never gone beyond a certain boundary. Alice had always thought what people did in the privacy of their homes was their business. Apparently this was a business to the Filipovs. The women and some of the men were prostitutes. It was nothing Alice hadn't seen before, but the memories it conjured up disgusted her. She was tempted to just go in and start shooting, but she saw none of the other faces she would recognize

from The Assemblage and she wanted to get as many as she could. She'd have to wait for their 'party.'

Alice stole food to keep her and Sasha alive. Living in the barn was tricky. They couldn't be seen so they had hidden their baggage, but they were living it rough. The lack of bathing was the worst. Hay, straw, and its dust were in their clothes and everywhere on their skin. Their hair was a mess and Alice, for once, appreciated the short hair, but it was growing rapidly. She wanted to cut it again, but that would have to wait. Sasha had never roughed it like this. The only time it had been worse for her was in prison. She kept her mind on the goal of making each member of The Assemblage pay.

Alice spent the time working on some metal she had brought with them. Sasha learned to make a belt from it, but the shapes were really odd to her. She thought it clever that Alice made them fit within themselves, but the edges were so sharp that she worried they would cut themselves. They had to wear their gloves so that they didn't slice their hands.

"I wish I had my sharpener," Alice muttered more than once as they used a file on the edges of the links.

"You do zis often?" the Russian asked, curious.

"No, but I have an electric sharpener at home," she answered, although at this point, with Kathy thinking her dead, maybe she didn't any longer. She shrugged philosophically…things could be replaced.

Alice practiced in the loft whenever one of the farmers or workers weren't around. Her aim was off and that bothered her, but given that she hadn't used knives in a long time, that was to be expected. Sasha was impressed despite the inaccuracy.

They were there several days before they noted cars driving up the long driveway onto the farm. The night of the party must have arrived. A new batch of men and women had been bused in for the night.

"How will we handle this?" Sasha asked.

"I don't know," Alice confessed.

"You don't know?

Shrugging, she answered, "We will have to play this by ear."

Alice saw one of the farmers take his family and drive off the farm. She figured he didn't want to subject his family to the perversions that his employers indulged in on a regular basis when they were in residence. Alice knew that the Filipovs had several homes including this farm and another in Moscow.

"Let's go take a shower and change our clothes," she offered to Sasha who greedily accepted the proposition. They even had time to wash their dirty clothes. A washing machine was a luxury out here, but they were thrilled to find one and be able to use it. Sasha never doubted Alice's skill as she went to pick the lock on the farmer's house only to find it unlocked. Such trusting people! They cleaned up and ate a hot meal, the first in a week, grateful for the farmer who had left. Before the night was in full swing, they were back in their barn, hidden and waiting.

"I see Kozlov," Sasha confessed from the position she was in, using a telescope to watch the arriving guests.

Alice nodded, knowing that this woman was on their list.

"I see Pajari," Alice noted a while later as she took a turn.

That was at least three more on their list, but they were hoping to see the Baltizars—one or more of them. They were at the head of The Assemblage from what they had learned. The many documents on the computer told them so.

"I hate to tell you, but our white faces can be seen clearly in the moonlight," Alice mentioned to Sasha.

"We finally just got showers and now you want us to dirty them up?" Sasha complained good-naturedly. She sighed, Alice was probably right…she was always right.

Alice went down to get some dirt using her penlight and shielding it from the main house so no one would become curious. Sasha followed and watched as Alice rubbed the dirt on her cheeks and forehead to hide the glare of her pale white skin.

Sasha reached down without the penlight to rub some on her own face. "This stinks," she complained, wrinkling her nose.

Alice shined the penlight on her friend and then burst out in laughter. At Sasha's questioning glare she confessed, "That isn't dirt you just rubbed all over your face."

Horrified, Sasha looked at her hands. When Alice shined the light on them, she could see the tell-tale signs of some sort of animal dung on them. "Oh, God, I think I'm going to be sick," she confessed and heaved a little.

"Just use the trough and try again," Alice advised, still trying to hide her amusement at her friend's predicament.

Sasha did as Alice suggested, feeling sick to her stomach that she had animal shit on her hands and face. In her enthusiasm to copy Alice, she had really smeared it all over the white of her face. She was sure the water, which was freezing cold, didn't get it all off. She probably had it in her hair too. She gulped to hide the smell that was prevalent in her nostrils. Once she had washed it off, Alice made sure to apply real dirt. They both lamented the fact that just a few hours ago they had a hot shower and a good meal and now they were dirty once again.

Alice put a rucksack on her back to carry things she thought she might need. They began to make their way up to the house. More and more cars

had arrived while they were showering and cleaning up and now they could see them parked all over haphazardly.

"Do you think they will have a computer here?" Sasha asked as they waited, for what, neither of them knew.

Alice shrugged. "It wouldn't matter if they did out here." She was remembering the service they didn't have back in the village.

Sasha agreed, she was just making conversation to make the time go by. She was excited and yet worried that they would get caught.

"We should scope this out more," Alice murmured as they gazed through the windows with the goggles and the telescope. "We haven't been to the other side of the house."

To waste time they hiked around the large house, noting the windows and doors and their placement. Alice pointed these things out to Sasha in case they should become separated and need to escape. As they came to the far side of the house, they noted a set of sheds, side by side. Alice made her way there, noticing a strange odor. Glancing back at the big house she decided to risk lighting her penlight. She wished she hadn't when she found a vat in the first shed.

"What is that?" Sasha asked over her shoulder as she blocked the light from being seen in the house on the hill.

Alice shone the light around inside the vat and nearly vomited. It was human remains, floating in what looked like a soup. She quickly put the lid down and flicked the light around. The odor was nauseating! They were using the remains as a compost. Whatever the pigs didn't eat must go out on the fields. Alice was horrified. Never, in all her years—and she had seen a lot—had she found something so repugnantly disgusting.

"What *is* that?" Sasha asked again and Alice explained, trying to keep the good dinner they had earlier from coming back up. Sasha couldn't

keep hers down as she realized what she had seen. Both of them hopped backwards from the splash at their feet as Sasha threw up. "Are you sure?"

At Alice's nod, Sasha closed her eyes trying to un-see what she had seen, but it was impossible. "Now what do we do?" she asked instead, swallowing spasmodically, trying to distract herself.

"How do you feel about actually killing someone yourself?" Alice asked. Up until now, Alice had been the one doing all the killing. Sasha had been a font of information, but maybe now that had changed.

"I don't know," she confessed honestly, but after what she had seen since she had found out these people had stolen from her and from others—including life—she wasn't so sure she couldn't.

"Well, here," Alice said taking the nail gun from her rucksack. "This is the safety button...just point and click." She showed her, and after a couple of practices without actually shooting the nails Sasha felt comfortable enough with the weapon that she might be able to slide off the safety switch. "Do not point it at anything or anyone you don't mean to fire at," Alice warned. "Especially me," she added to bring some levity to the situation. They were walking away from the sheds, putting distance between them and the horrifying sight and smell. Both would have to work hard to not see again what they had already seen.

"Why do these people do things like that?" Sasha asked, naively.

"Greed mostly. Many times they have this superior sense of self. They don't think the law can touch them. Here, they own the law." Both of them had read the payoff amounts. They paid a lot of police, politicians, and others to keep their activities secret. "But they also have a flaw in their makeup. They are perverted or perhaps just crazy."

Sasha almost asked if Alice was one of those. Her ability to kill unnerved Sasha, but at the same time if someone like Alice didn't exist, Sasha wouldn't be here to take the revenge she needed to.

"I just bring them justice," Alice finished as they began to walk around the house again, almost reading Sasha's mind. They were careful to stay far enough out that servants and guests alike would not see them.

The party was well-established and neither of the unwelcome guests knew the timing or how to start their own party. It was started for them when a guest and his partner drunkenly stumbled out on the large patio. It was too cold for what they had planned, but both were inebriated enough that they thought they could manage. The woman managed to slip away laughingly, too cold to let the natural order of events continue, and running playfully back inside.

The man, angry at her escape, decided not to waste his erection and began to jerk off. He never noticed as Alice crept up on him and sliced open his throat. Both she and Sasha looked down as his blood soaked into his fine suit. They recognized him from his pictures. It was Kozlov.

Alice thought for a minute what the name Kozlov meant—goatherd or something. The translation wasn't exact. The man sort of did look like a goat with his goatee. "Help me," she whispered to Sasha and grabbed a leg to pull the man out of the light from the windows reflecting on the patio. They soon had him behind some bushes. 'One down,' thought Alice. There were many to go.

"What, do we wait for these people to come out? One at a time?" Sasha grouched quietly, her feet stamping in the cold.

"Well, do you have an idea?" Alice asked. They certainly weren't dressed for a party in their jeans and sweat shirts with their coats on over

them. Their boots, while warm, were losing their ability to hold that warmth by standing too long in one place.

"Uh oh," Sasha answered instead. The party was spilling out onto the patio and backyard. The two women hid behind some bushes to watch. Servants had come out with heaters and blowers so that the guests could make use of the area. The two women exchanged looks, wondering how long it would take someone to find Kozlov's body. It was amazing how an army of servants, including prostitutes, could transform an area into a festive occasion. Christmas lights were soon strung, decorations abounded, alcohol was flowing from a bar, and guests were flowing from inside to outside.

"We should watch the front too," Alice fretted. She could see a couple of the guests leaving already and she didn't want to miss this opportunity to get anyone from The Assemblage if they could.

"I'm staying here," Sasha asserted firmly. She had just spotted Vashti Baltizar and Alice followed her intense look to see him too.

"Don't do anything unless he is alone," Alice told her firmly. She was torn between going to the front of the house and staying to help. Sasha could easily get them both caught and she didn't want that. After all the annoying time together, she considered the woman a friend. It was then that they both heard a loud voice. Pajari was enjoying herself a bit much over the ledge of an open window from upstairs. Someone was obviously doing her from behind. Her breasts hung over the ledge and she had a champagne glass in her hand. She was squeaking in delight as she moved with the thrusts. Alice and Sasha both squatted to keep from being seen. "Give me the nail gun," Alice said firmly.

Sasha had been about to try, even with someone behind the woman. This woman was the one they had determined that had filmed Lexi's beating. Her voice was imprinted on Sasha's mind. She'd recognize it

anywhere. Sasha looked at Alice's intent look, her hand held out, and without a qualm handed her the nail gun. She watched as Alice, keeping down low below the bushes, maneuvered herself into a position below the woman hanging out the upstairs window.

"Merry Christmas! Merry Christmas!" Pajari was calling in both Russian and Finnish. She was oblivious to the fact that her breasts were hanging down and slapping against the ledge. She raised her glass to salute those who might look up at her antics and laugh. The few souls out in the cold from the overcrowded house soon returned to their own conversations or groping. Some even returned inside, leaving the few servants outside to serve whoever might brave the cold.

This was what Alice was waiting for. Less witnesses, less chance of being seen. It sounded like Pajari was nearing a climax. Alice took aim with the nail gun and slid off the safety. Just as the woman drank the last of her champagne, gulping it and tossing down the glass—its tinkle was heard as it broke on the patio stone—Alice fired off not one, but two nails. Both struck home. The woman's shriek would be thought to be one of ecstasy. Her slumping over the edge of the window would cause a few moments delay before her partner would realize she was not overcome by passion, but was actually dead.

Alice quickly looked around, checking if anyone had seen her and started to make her way back to Sasha, not feeling good about leaving the woman alone. She was just in time to shoot the nail gun another time. Their hostess, Galina Filipov, was even now stalking Sasha. Galina had caught the woman stealing a couple of candy canes from their decorations. Sasha had thought herself unobserved until the woman called her name, sharply and with anger.

"You think, Brenhov, we don't know that you are in Russia? We knew! But that you would kill, this isn't what we expected. You can't be doing this yourself? You would get your nails dirty," she scoffed. She never anticipated the nail through her back.

Alice had aimed carefully, hitting the spine and severing it, but not killing the woman. She watched dispassionately as the woman went down.

"Give me that," Sasha said imperiously, holding her hand out for the nail gun.

"Wait, let's do to her what she has done to others," Alice said meaningfully.

Sasha looked at her a moment and then glanced down at the gasping woman. The shock of the injury kept the woman quiet; she couldn't move. She could, however, hear them and pleaded to both of them with her eyes. Realizing what Alice might mean, Sasha nodded. The woman deserved no less.

"Help me," Alice told the woman and between them they got Galina up and managed to carry her, with frequent rests, to the barn on the other side of the house. Both were perspiring from the exertion. They did, however, make it to the boar pens where the pigs realized someone was about. They began to squeal in their excitement. The noise was deafening. "Hurry," Alice gasped, trying to exert more strength from her body. Without Sasha's help she would never have been able to get the woman to the pen, much less over the high side. The weight of the boars as they reared up was causing the wood to bow outwards. Both women exchanged a look before a last heave had them throwing Galina over. The pigs' noises were horrific and they quickly left the pen. "Let's get our stuff. We're done here," Alice told Sasha.

"But what about Filipov's husband? What about Vashti Baltizar? There are others…" Sasha protested.

"We have to take what we can get," Alice told her as she headed for the ladder.

"And so do I," said a voice, menacingly.

Both women looked up and could see a figure standing there in the darkness. The little light in the barn reflected off what was clearly a gun. They exchanged a look that neither could see in the darkness.

"You two are the ones that The Assemblage has been looking for," he said matter-of-factly. "Uh uh," he said to Alice as she made to make a move. His gun waved and she could see it. He would shoot. She didn't doubt that at the moment. "I want to thank you for getting rid of that bitch," he continued. They could all still hear the boars feasting on the woman they had thrown into the pen…the guttural sounds were sickening. "I'll inherit everything now. No more will I be kept on a leash." He meant it literally as well as figuratively.

They both realized they were facing Filpov's husband, the letch who had felt Alice up in the bar.

Alice's mind was working quickly, but she didn't know if she could throw her links in the dark. She knew her accuracy was off. A gun only required a pulling of the trigger and a pointing. Knives required accuracy.

"Both of you, walk over there," he said. They had to peer in the darkness to see where he was waving. Away from the barn, to the far side out by the cattle. "Get going," he told them, pushing on Sasha who almost stumbled trying to walk among the cow patties.

It had rained one of the days they had been hiding on the farm and since then it had snowed. The ground was slippery and both women had a hard time walking. Fortunately, the moon had risen and lit their way.

"Over there," he directed again and they were led up to a hole in the ground. Both blanched. It was dug recently, and was the perfect size for a grave.

"You see, we had intended to lose a friend today," he began conversationally to explain the hole in his cow field. "I think, Brenhov, you were a friend once," he laughed evilly. He adjusted himself on the ground to get a firm stance so he could kill not just one of them, but both. It was as he lifted his foot that he slipped.

It was what Alice was waiting for. Her hand moved rapidly and she threw one of the discs from her belt. Her aim was off, but as he was slipping at the same time and unbalanced, she managed to nick him alongside his cheek in a deep gouge that immediately began to bleed. The gun went off, but his aim was way off. "Come on," Alice shouted at Sasha.

The two of them charged the man and Sasha got to him first. She knocked into him like a football player, taking him down. He had been unsteady on his feet already, but her charge left him falling. He hit his head and then his hand, knocking the gun from his grip. Alice picked up the gun. The man was unconscious. Putting the gun's safety on, she slipped it into her pocket.

"Come on," she repeated and Sasha saw her grab a pants' leg. Between the two of them they yanked him closer to the hole before rolling him in. He hit the bottom of the hole with a thud.

"Are we going to bury him?" Sasha asked, stupidly. She was stunned with how rapidly this had gone.

There were two shovels standing in the pile of loose soil, Alice indicated them to Sasha. "That's not frozen yet." She grabbed one of the shovels.

"What about that shot? Won't that bring someone?" Sasha asked, but followed Alice's lead and grabbed the other shovel.

"With as much partying as is going on up there, I doubt it," she said as she dug into the loose dirt and went to shovel it into the hole.

Sasha followed suit and threw her shovelful on his face. He woke up and looked up in alarm. It took a few more shovels full of dirt before he realized where he was. He immediately tried to get up and out of the grave where they were burying him alive. Sasha hit him with her shovel, right over the head, and down he went again, stunned.

The two of them worked quickly and in no time the body was covered. They continued until it was quite deeply buried, transferring the loose soil to the grave. They didn't finish completely, both were too tired for that, but he was already under several feet of dirt. They threw in a few rocks and then left the grave.

"Let's get our things," Alice said once again and headed for the barn and their bags.

"Steal a car?" Sasha asked, unnecessarily as she took her own bags from Alice.

"Sounds good," she answered. Alice wondered how Sasha felt about what she herself had done this evening. The woman had never killed before, not by herself. Alice felt no remorse, but then she had done this before. Right now, Alice was betting that Sasha was in shock.

"It's Vashti," she gasped, seeing someone staggering out to a car. He opened the car door and the light splashed against his white skin and white hair.

"Wait," Alice cautioned her, seeing her moving to get to the bag that contained the nail gun.

It was too late; the man had seen them. "Sasha? Sasha Brenhov?" the albino man asked, incredulously, turning from the car door. "That was you in Dubai too, wasn't it?" he accused.

"Yes, you bastard, it was. You think you and your family can just get away with putting me in prison?" she spat out, wishing she had Alice's knife and making a mental note she would never be unprotected again.

He laughed. "Has it been you taking out The Assemblage?" he wondered aloud. "I was sure you had hired assassins," he slurred. He was weaving from side to side. He glanced at Alice, wondering who she was. "Who's this? Your *girl*friend?" He put enough insinuation into it to make it an insult.

"Just because I didn't wish to date your brother..." she began, but had to jump back as he vomited on the ground near his car. She stared at him in disgust as he pulled himself together.

"You like *girls*..." he spat out, wiping his lips with the back of his hand.

"Not all girls. Just one in particular..." she began defensively.

"Ah, yes, the beautiful Alexis," he stated with a gleam in his eye. He grinned evilly. "We will have everything soon," he informed her. "Maybe I'll teach her what a real man–" he didn't finish as Sasha launched herself at him.

Sasha didn't think, she just knew instant rage at the thought that he would touch Alexis. Not he, nor anyone else, would ever touch her Lexi...never! She had no formal training, but she threw herself at him, clawing at his face, her nail cutting down his cheek.

"You bitch," he yelled as he threw her from him. He was then knocked against his car as Alice entered the fray.

Seeing Sasha so easily thrown from the man, Alice dropped their bags and centered a high kick into his chest. Not only was he totally

unprepared for the attack, but he was an easy target. She effortlessly bounced off his chest as he came in contact with his car door, his back hitting the edge of the open door. "You like hit woman, you try me," she said imperfectly in Russian.

"Ah, who is this?" he asked, eyeing the smaller, petite woman with interest. His back was smarting from the car door, but his drunken state ensured he wasn't feeling it fully. "Is this the dyke you've been traveling with?" He glanced down at Sasha who was slowly getting up from the ground and went after Alice.

"I may a dyke be, but I be more woman than you handle," Alice told him.

"Really? Come on bitch," he motioned and then was actually shocked when she did.

Having gloves on, Alice knew her hands were fairly protected. She brought them up and punched the man, knowing he wouldn't expect a woman to attack in such a masculine way. A quick, one-two jab and his nose was bleeding, broken from the crunch they all heard.

Vashti looked down at his hand as it pulled away from his nose, the blood made him blink in his inebriated state. Unfortunately, the pain from his back and from his nose didn't register completely due to the alcohol in his system. He glanced down and saw drips of blood on his white shirt. He looked up at his attacker. "You bitch! You ruined my Brooks Brothers' shirt!" he told her angrily.

Alice didn't stop. Bringing up both hands, she clapped them over his ears. Knowing the man was bigger and stronger, she knew she had to be quick about her attack. All it would take is one blow from him to lessen her defenses. The loss of his equilibrium from the hand clap had him

bending over. She kneed him in the face hearing another crunch from his nose. She backed off as he tried to reach for her, bouncing on her toes.

Sasha had pulled herself up and was watching the fight. She had seen Alice practicing, but she thought it was for exercise. It had never occurred to her that the woman would actually physically attack someone. She didn't know she had skills like this. Watching Vashti bleed was immensely satisfying. She put her hands in her coat pockets to watch.

"What the hell is going on here?" another voice yelled at them and Sasha turned to see Leonid Baltizar coming towards them. He was bigger and angrier than his brother, Vashti. His white hair, kept at shoulder length, gleamed in the moonlight. His albinoism was compounded by a red birth mark on his forehead. The combination made for a very ugly man. He reached in his pocket and Sasha attacked with her only defense.

Sasha had picked up two of the candy canes used in decoration on the patio with the intention of eating them later. That was how Galina Filipov had caught her. She pulled them out of her pocket now, looked at them both in her fist, and remembered Alice using the icicles. She plunged them both into Leonid Baltizar's neck. They had blunt ends, but his rushing towards Alice and Vashti's fight and ignoring Sasha, allowed the impetus of his stride to impale the candy canes deeply in his neck. He looked at Sasha in horror, his hand going to his neck. He pulled one of the canes from his neck and looked at it in astonishment as it dripped blood. He looked over it at Sasha for a moment. She thought he was going to come after her and she took a step back, slipping on the snow and falling to the ground. She watched as though in slow motion as he knelt to the snow and fell beside her. She quickly rolled away from him and got up on her feet, looking at Alice to see if she had seen what Sasha had done.

Alice had just pulled one of the links from her belt and in a slashing movement, cut along Vashti's neck. He pulled back further, his nose and

neck bleeding profusely. Alice spun, slipped slightly on the snow, causing her well-aimed kick to hit his chest instead of his jaw. They all heard the crunch as he turned from the kick, hitting the edge of his car door with his head. He slid down the black BMW to the snow where a pool of blood began to spill out.

Alice was breathing hard, but she managed to put the link back in her belt as she bent over Vashti, glancing at Sasha in surprise. "Who is that?" she asked, pointing with her chin at the other albino. She could tell he was a Baltizar, but she didn't know which one.

"This was Leonid," Sasha answered woodenly, still in shock over what she had done as she gestured to the fallen man.

Alice was going through the pockets of Vashti.

"What are you doing?"

Alice glanced over at the candy cane sticking out of Leonid's neck. "I'm looking for his keys. We have to get out of here." She soon found them in his pocket along with his identification and cell phone. She took them both, pushing a button on the key to unlock the trunk. "Help me," she ordered Sasha as she took one pants' leg and began to pull him along the slippery ground.

"What are you doing?" Sasha repeated.

"Getting rid of the bodies. Sending a message," she mumbled the last part.

With much heaving, Sasha helped her to put Vashti in the trunk of the car. She then had Alice help her with Leonid's body. She was amazed that two fully grown men fit in the trunk of the car.

"So much blood, so little time," Alice quipped. There was a lot of blood on the ground. The snow was covering it up, but the drag marks were obvious. She wiped a bit of blood from the back of the car with

snow. She then searched Leonid's pockets for anything she could use. She pocketed his wallet and phone and found nothing more. Alice closed the trunk. "Come on," she told Sasha. "Get in the car. Be careful you don't step in the blood." Alice quickly packed their bags in the back seat.

They were both a bit of a mess. Dirt was all over their clothes and blood too. The BMW purred to life and they slowly drove away. Alice was mindful of the road. It was slick and she didn't need an accident, not now, especially with two bodies in the trunk.

Alice glanced over at Sasha and adjusted the heat in the car, turning it up. She could see the woman was shaking. "Are you okay?" she asked after a while.

"I'm cold," Sasha admitted, rubbing her arms, grateful for the heat.

"We're going to have to stop somewhere and clean up," Alice mentioned as she drove through the village and headed for the highway. The snowfall was increasing, making the roads slipperier.

"Where are we going?"

"I don't know," she admitted with a shrug.

"Maybe we should go back and use that farm worker's house," she mentioned.

"Too late now," she sounded regretful that she hadn't thought of it herself.

"Gawd, I can't get warm," Sasha complained and looked around the car. In the back seat was a blanket and overcoat. "Oh, good," she mumbled as she reached for both. She covered herself with the blanket first and then the overcoat.

"Careful," Alice said, eying the overcoat thoughtfully. She drove for a while, noticing the gas tank was quite full and grateful for it. As they came to a larger town, she saw a hotel. She slowed the car.

"What are you doing?" Sasha asked. They had been quiet for most of the trip and she was finally warm from the efficient heating system of the car and the blanket. She'd stopped shaking and for that alone she was grateful.

"We need to clean up," Alice mentioned again and pulled up to register. She pulled the overcoat to her and struggled to get into it. Looking in the mirror, she tried to rub most of the dirt from her face. Leaving the car running with Sasha in it, she got out and adjusted the overcoat to hide her dirty and bloody clothes. She went inside.

The proprietor looked at her strangely, but her money was good even if her Russian wasn't. He could tell she was a foreigner, but her passport was good so he rented her a room. Alice didn't make any special requests. She wanted to raise no questions. She thanked him and gave him a smile.

"You got it?" Sasha asked, rhetorically, as Alice got back in the car and drove to the parking in front of the hotel. It was in view of the office and Alice thought perhaps that was on purpose.

"Only grab your bag with the clothes," she told Sasha as she turned off the car.

Sasha listened to her without question as she opened the back door and pulled out her bag.

Alice glanced around, grateful that the owner couldn't see Sasha on the far side of the car. She looked terrible with blood on her and dirt on both her face and clothes. Alice quickly locked the BMW and unlocked the room. "You take a shower first," she offered.

Sasha accepted gratefully. She rummaged through her clothes, wishing she had more, and remembering how she took for granted the full closets she used to have. She headed into the small bathroom and peeled off the clothes she had been wearing.

"Don't throw those out," Alice called to caution her.

"Why not?"

"We'll wash them. We may have a use for them again."

Sasha nodded as she closed the door to give herself some privacy. Alice always thought ahead like that. Personally, she would have tossed them. The blood on them made her shudder. Then she saw the remnants of the manure she had used on herself. She hadn't been able to get the stench out of her nostrils since the farm, but she must have become used to it. She gratefully got under the hot spray and began to wash.

Alice went through both wallets. Both men had carried large sums of cash, but Vashti had something else. She recognized it as a key to a vault in Switzerland. She wondered at its significance. It might just be a safety deposit box, but it might be something that would tell them more about The Assemblage. After going through their wallets thoroughly, she kept their cash, identification, and credit cards. She dissected their phones and, keeping the small card aside, she carefully crushed both phones; she'd dispose of them later. Without a body to prove they were dead, they and their money could be useful. Without their phones to track them—the cards were not active without the phones—they could be anywhere.

Alice thought for a moment and then went to fire up the laptop. They hadn't been able to use it on the farm and then she realized that this hotel had no internet access. She cursed her luck. They needed to get out for a while. There had been too many bodies for too long and she and Sasha needed to lay low for a while. She'd worry about that tomorrow.

Alice was grateful when Sasha finally finished in the bathroom so she too could shower. She took the time to wash her hair three times, grateful for the hot water and the clean soap. She finally got out and a billow of steam followed her when she opened the bathroom. She found Sasha lying on her bed. "Are you okay?" she asked, kindly.

Sasha blinked, sat up, and looked at Alice. "How can you be so calm?"

Alice shrugged. "I've seen a lot over the years," she confided.

"What do we do now?"

"I think we need to find a way to get rid of the cars and the bodies without touching either. I also think with so many of The Assemblage dying, we should stop for a while."

"Stop? I'm not going to stop until we get every one of those dogs!" Sasha said fiercely, the Tatars back in her Russian heritage rising up, ready for a battle.

Alice smiled. "I need a break, and your Russian winter is upon us. I think we should go somewhere warm for a while."

The mention of 'warm' appealed to Sasha too. In all the years of her deal-making she hadn't thought about a Russian winter. She'd been too busy living the cushy life to worry about staying warm, or about people like this who had obviously targeted them.

"Are you going to steal their accounts too?" she asked, her head nodding towards where the car was parked and her hand vaguely gesturing to those they had killed that night.

"We will, but I think it would be better to do it from afar. How does Dubai sound about now?"

Remembering how warm it had been there in that desert country, Sasha thought it sounded wonderful. "Will we be able to access…" she began to ask. Then she worried about the Baltizar family when they realized that two of their own were missing.

"We should be able to and I'll work extra hard to trace those we just took care of," Alice promised as she got into her own bed in preparation for sleep.

"I'm hungry," Sasha noted.

"If you could, order something…" Alice mentioned sleepily as she laid back.

Sasha nodded. She could see Alice was tired. She was too, but she was still a little wired from their evening's activities. She looked at the clock and realized nothing was open. She would have to wait for morning. She glanced over at Alice. Already her eyes were shut, but she wasn't asleep. Sighing gustily, she'd gone without so many times this past year or so, she could afford to miss this meal. She got into bed herself and tried to go to sleep. She had troubled dreams though, as she remembered killing Leonid Baltizar over and over in her mind. She had to remember it was self-defense. It was either him or her and she had prevailed. She wondered if he would have had trouble sleeping if he had managed to kill her? She glanced frequently over at Alice who didn't seem to have trouble sleeping. It was then she began to remember they had buried a man alive this night. Her own lack of sleep allowed her time to imagine how it would be to smother to death that way. She looked again at Alice who was soundly sleeping.

Sasha was wrong. Alice was having trouble sleeping, she just didn't show it. Her conscience was clear over killing those people tonight, they had deserved it. What was troubling her was thoughts of Kathy and the kids and how she was going to get back to them. This wasn't going to be an easy fix and she worried that it would take far too long to get home. Kathy might have moved on, even married. She certainly had no reason to mourn Alice forever. They hadn't had a chance to make up from their separation, she had no reason to wait for her.

~ ~ ~ ~ ~

"I did mourn you," Kathy confided, interrupting her story.

"I worried about you constantly," Alice answered, her hand caressing along Kathy's face. Almost as though she were memorizing it again.

"You came back to me," Kathy answered, pleased with the touch. She had missed it. She had craved it. She welcomed Alice's touch. She also felt a jolt of desire and pushed it down. Until she knew it all, it was inappropriate. "Please go on," she asked, regretfully. She needed to know.

Alice smiled. She would have liked a break, but telling Kathy the whole story was, she knew, a necessary evil. Kathy deserved to know why she had stayed away so long. She could have glossed over the details, but she was her wife, she knew what Alice was, she deserved the truth.

~ ~ ~ ~ ~

Alice got up late the next morning and stretched. She could see Sasha was still asleep. She could also see by the messed up bedclothes that the woman hadn't had a restful night. She wasn't surprised. Murdering someone, even in self-defense, was not easy. To Alice it was just a necessary evil. They hadn't deserved to live. She just thought about those people briefly and then moved on mentally. She did make a mental note to probe further into their finances. She especially wanted to know more about that remote farm. She wondered how many of those prostitutes would actually be free now that their 'masters' were dead? Had anyone found the dead woman in the bedroom? The one in the pigs' pen? The buried man? Had the alarm been raised yet?

Alice looked for and found a menu she could order from. Using her phone in the bathroom, she ordered a large breakfast as she used the facilities. She was pleased that her Russian had improved enough that she

not only understood it, but could speak it reasonably well, if imperfectly. She liked that she and Sasha now conversed in it regularly, but she knew her Russian was probably as faulty as Sasha's English.

Later, while Sasha took a nap, Alice found a laundromat and was able to wash their bloody and dirty clothes. She put them through several cycles before allowing the stained clothes to dry. After her shower, she had put the bloody clothes in cold water to soak overnight, but even with that, some of the stains would not come out completely. She was pleased that only she could really see them, but then, she was looking for them.

Sasha had eaten most of their breakfast when it arrived, not realizing that Alice had left it to go wash their clothes. This annoyed the American a bit, but she hadn't left a note, only the money to pay for their delivery. For all Sasha had known, the entire delivery was for her alone. Alice quickly caught up. She was ravenous too after the lean pickings on the farm.

~ ~ ~ ~ ~

They drove all the way back to Moscow…it took forever. Russia was a vast country and people tended to forget the huge distances between cities and towns. It was more populated in the eastern part of the country, nearer to Europe, but even this was spread out.

"It is worse when you go to Siberia," Sasha pointed out when they discussed the distances in Russia versus the USA.

Alice deliberately drove the expensive BMW into a poorer part of Moscow. She left the keys on the floor and the doors unlocked as Sasha waited for her back at the subway station. She hoped the car would be stolen, stripped, and—once the bodies were found—taken care of *for* them. Alice hiked back to where she left Sasha and the two of them took

the subway to the airport. Alice had purchased two tickets to Dubai using the credit cards of the Baltizar brothers on behalf of their 'girlfriends.' They still had to show identification so they used their original passports. Willow and Lorraine were going to have a good time on the Baltizar brothers while they could. Alice had also started looking into how much was on their credit cards. She would max them out when she could by not only paying for their hotel stays in Dubai, but taking cash advances. She wanted everyone to think that the brothers had taken girls on a vacation and were just out of reach. She was willing to bet that these two were a bit irresponsible, or rather she was hoping they were. She would purchase a couple of phones there and slip the cards into them, the ping from the phones would give their location and legitimize their credit card charges.

As they left their bags in a storage locker near the airport, Alice wondered if arriving in Dubai without luggage would arouse anyone's suspicions. As they went through security, her belt did set off an alarm. She took it off with a charming smile and security scanned it, saw nothing wrong with the metal belt, and cleared Lorraine Brown. Willow Wentworth had no problem either with her carry-on bag containing their laptop and the two of them breathed a sigh of relief as their plane took off for Dubai.

Once in Dubai and through security, they went, not directly to their hotel, but to the Dubai Mall in downtown Burj. Although she had never been there, Alice had read up on the mall and found it was the most frequented shopping mall. She figured they could stock up on clothes and finally feel normal again. Sasha had been to Dubai and the mall, and she was able to direct them to several stores. The Baltizars' credit cards were well used by the time the two women finished shopping. They not only had a nice set of luggage each, but the clothes to fill them, including casual

and formal attire. They both had their hair done while they were there, going back to their own particular shades of blonde. Then they checked into their hotel where Vashti, unknowingly, had rented them a suite. If he had known what a nice place Alice had chosen, he would have chosen it himself and never found Willow in the other hotel. He hadn't wanted to be seen or accidentally found at the time anyway.

The two of them stayed a week in that hotel and by then they were both tanned, rested, and feeling 'warm.' Alice also determined that the Baltizar family had tracked their wayward sons to Dubai by way of their credit cards, phone pings, and 'girlfriends' and she decided the two of them should make themselves scarce. Using their own credit cards under their various aliases, they were able to make a change to another hotel. Before they left, Alice used their excellent internet service to max out the credit cards with their high limits and the cash helped pad both women's pockets. They destroyed the cards, the phones and their incriminating as well as traceable cards, and discarded them after that.

The second week in the different hotel was spent relaxing some more. Alice could discern the increasing alarm over the Baltizar brothers' disappearance from the Filipov farm from the emails that she was intercepting. Only occasionally did the programs fail to give her a direct translation and she would have to ask Sasha to read them all to translate. While in Dubai, she stopped at a couple of computer stores for programs she knew she could use. She longed for her bank of computers back home in Palos Verdes, but stifled any and all thoughts of home or her family. She lay beside the pool, soaking up the sun, and tanning as she contemplated how to get rid of more of The Assemblage and their ilk.

"They are on to us," Sasha stated after reading an email of some length from one of the members of The Assemblage to another.

"They've been on to us for a while," Alice answered thoughtfully. This would make it harder to find these people as they scattered across Russia and possibly the world. Alice had to admit some of it she enjoyed...the hunt was proving interesting.

~ ~ ~ ~ ~

"Do you own a gold mine?" Alice asked as she looked at some of the activity they were keeping track of.

"Yes, we own two," Sasha admitted without shame, looking up from the magazine she was reading. She wondered what Alice had found. "Also oil, gas, and..." she began to repeat conversations they had had over the year.

Alice held up her hand to silence the platinum blonde. "What do you think this means?" she asked, pointing at the emails she was comparing to banking information.

Sasha got up and squinted at the information Alice was reviewing. "This is Olimpiada, it's in Severo-Yenyseisk, Krasnoyarsk Krai District," she pointed to a map Alice had up too. "The other one is in Blagodatnoye, Krasnoyarsk Region, in Eastern Siberia," she informed her, the Russian names flowing effortlessly over her tongue.

Alice nodded as she began to get a better picture of the layout of the Brenhov enterprises. "They are trying to buy these from Alexis," she pointed out the email concerning the gold interests.

"My Lexi, she knows those make a lot of money for me," Sasha said affectionately, obviously missing the American woman who was her lover and who had inherited her vast fortune.

"So she wouldn't sell?"

"I don't know," Sasha faltered as she thought it over. Alexis might sell just to get rid of her ties to Russia. Especially with the persuasion that had been used on her before, in the form of a beating. She was a staunch American, stubborn, unwilling to leave America except for occasional trips abroad. Sasha had wanted to move her in with her and to travel with her always, but the woman had refused, refusing to be 'kept.' Stubborn woman! "She has sold a few things I didn't think she would," she murmured musingly. It was also something that she may have been forced to do.

"I really don't want to go to Siberia if we don't have to," Alice said jokingly. From the comfort of their hotel suite in Dubai, the heat, the sun, and the mini-vacation they had allowed themselves, it was a far cry from the cold steppes of Russia's Siberia, much less the cold mountains where the mines were located.

"The mines here," she indicated Severo-Yenyseisk, "are next to a river." She showed on the map exactly where. Severo-Yenyseisk is one of forty-three districts in Krasnoyarsk Krai. The other one," she moved her finger on the map, "is a small operation here," she showed Blagodatnoye in the Krasnoyarsk region, in Eastern Siberia. "They have tried to buy it—" she began, only to be interrupted by Alice.

"Who is they?"

"Polyus Gold International owns the largest mines in the area including Blagodatnoye. It's like a strip-mine. I wouldn't be surprised if The Assemblage is trying to get a foothold in the area by acquiring my family's holdings and then going after Polyus."

Alice quickly pulled up information on Polyus and read that Blagodatnoye was only their second largest mine in Russia and that they produced the most gold in Russia. It would be a very valuable asset for The Assemblage to acquire. It must be part of their long-term plans.

"This certainly would add to their holdings substantially," she pointed out. She made a mental note to invest in Polyus Gold herself after this was over. "It looks like they are making a move."

Sasha felt an overwhelming urge to go and protect her girlfriend. Alexis, or Lexi as she was called, would not be allowed to be beaten into selling Sasha's holdings, one by one. "We must do something," she stated unequivocally.

Alice had to agree, but they had to time it right to arrive when the remaining members of The Assemblage would be at one or both of the mines so that they could eliminate them. Already there were a couple of replacements in the hierarchy of The Assemblage. Alice needed an eye within their group to know what they were doing. So far no one had figured out that all their emails were being duplicated and sent to Alice's accounts. She'd used the keylogger programs to find the bank accounts, but she didn't have them all. Some of those she was targeting were a little more savvy about their computer systems. The company ones she hadn't even touched as extensively as their personal finances. She picked up one of the programs she knew would help her on the business systems. It would ghost their accounts, slowly diverting the actual funds until, when she was ready, she would make the ghosts disappear along with the company funds…bankrupting them. It would work slowly, insidiously, but be absolutely effective once she got into the remaining Assemblage members' computers. Even with firewalls in place, if they logged in from their home computers, she could ride along without anyone being aware of it. It was those that had firewalls and no outside access that she wanted to get into most. It was almost a challenge to her fertile mind. "It's time to go back," she sighed. All good vacations must come to an end. They had both needed this time off.

With their new clothing packed in their new luggage, the two women boarded a plane back to Moscow. Their intention was to make their way back to their car and Vologda. They never saw the man watching them leave the hotel, get in a taxi behind their own, or watch as they got in line to board the plane.

Their arrival in Moscow was normal. The customs agent didn't seem to notice the difference in their hair from redheads to blonde, but it could have been the push of an overwhelming number of passengers trying to get through customs. They took a taxi to their storage unit, collecting their other bags, and had the taxi take them to the train station. As they went to get the train to take them up to Vologda, they both felt the guns shoved into their backs.

"You will come with us," a voice said to both women.

Alice looked up to see the woman in front of them. She was one of the biggest women Alice had ever seen. She wasn't fat, just very muscular, massive, and tall. She had short hair in the form of a crew cut and a flat, Slavik face. She had a long scar along her jawline, almost as though someone had tried to cut off her face and had not succeeded. It was fairly recent, still pink, and not faded at all. It didn't detract from her face and Alice recognized the sturdily-built female guard from the prison. She glanced at Sasha, who also recognized the woman.

"And if I don't?" Alice asked in a smart-alecky voice.

The woman's eyes narrowed. "Ah, you *do* speak our language," she answered in a soft velvety-smooth voice.

"I do now."

"You didn't before?" She was surprised. She had been sure the woman back in Honduras had known more than she pretended.

Alice shook her head. "No, I didn't." She figured why not let them know she understood them now. It wouldn't change the fact that they had been caught.

It was obvious the woman didn't believe Alice. She made a gesture with her head and the guns shoved into the two women's backs pushed them along.

Alice thought about making a scene, sure they wouldn't want gunfire in public. Then, glancing at Sasha, she could tell the other woman was terrified. Seeing the guard from Honduras had unnerved her. She followed the large Russian woman, wondering if she would get a chance to bolt, and then her chances were lowered as they put handcuffs on first Alice and then Sasha. They were hustled into the back of a large, black car. The guard got in the front with the driver and the two who had held guns on Sasha and Alice got in the back with them. The car took off and the two prisoners were jostled against each other, trying unsuccessfully to hold their balance as they fell against each other. Alice tried to catch Sasha's eye, but the Russian was staring ahead, back in the stupor she had fallen into so long ago.

They were driven to a private airport, pulled from the car, and shoved and pushed onto a small jet. Here they were each chained with longer cuffs to a chair. *So much for getting out of the plane if they went down,* thought Alice. She watched her captors, who were taking particular care to talk in soft murmurs since it was obvious both of their captives understood them. Alice turned the chair as much as she could to try and catch Sasha's eye again. The woman seemed frozen. Trying to lift her leg to kick at the platinum blonde, she nearly yanked her arm out as the longer cuff chains were attached to her ankles too. Cursing their foresight, she was getting angry.

She'd been stupid to not realize that they would be watched for. After maxing out the Baltizar brothers' cards and taking a vacation to boot, she supposed that was thumbing their noses at those in The Assemblage. She wondered briefly if the BMW or their bodies had been found. She didn't really care, but she hadn't seen any of those types of emails concerning them since their disappearance.

Alice saw that their suitcases and bags were brought on board. She wondered if they had gone through them yet and saw they had not. They certainly weren't too concerned about them. She also wondered where they were going.

The Slavik woman returned from talking to someone in the front cabin, Alice assumed it was the captain. The door to the private plane was closed and the woman put a seat-belt across her lap. The two who had shoved their guns in Alice and Sasha's spines came from the forward cabin with drinks in hand and sat behind Alice and Sasha. Once they were up in the air, Alice watched, amused, as the woman whose name she idly wondered about, tried and failed to log onto Alice's laptop. The woman caught her watching and glared at her. Alice laughed aloud at the childish gesture. Settling back, she wondered again where they were going. They were obviously not going to tell the two women; they were ignored. Alice settled back and closed her eyes. She had watched movies on the flight from Dubai and enjoyed them immensely. She might as well get her sleep while she could. Who knew how long this flight would take.

~ ~ ~ ~ ~

Alice woke to the sound of the tires of the private plane hitting the ground. She looked out the windows, but in the dark couldn't see much except the blue lights of the edges of the runway. She wondered once

again where they were. As she lifted her hand to rub her nose sleepily, she was reminded that they had been captured when the cuff pulled at her wrist. She looked around to see the large woman getting up and stretching from the trip. She wished she knew what time it was; she had no idea. They hadn't patted the two women down so she still had her phone, her belt was still intact. Was it confidence in their abilities or sheer ignorance? She had no idea. She was interested in where they were taking them. She looked at Sasha who seemed to have snapped out of her trance. She looked at Alice with pleading, almost pathetic eyes. It was obvious she was frightened of whatever they would do or wherever they would take them.

Their leg shackles were taken off of them and the regular handcuffs, this time in front of them, were put back on. Another car was waiting for them. Their luggage as well as a few other extra items were all put in the trunk of the vehicle. The five of them were able to fit in the back. Alice found herself sitting next to the large woman and the two men sat on either side of Sasha. Alice looked at Sasha who tried to tell her something with her eyes.

Alice assumed the silence was supposed to unnerve them. Personally, she preferred the silence. She could tell that the two guards on either side of Sasha were uncomfortable. She observed each of the guards taking a finger to the inside collar of their suits on more than one occasion. It was then that she realized these two goons didn't wear them often and that these suits were new. She mentally laughed as she imagined they might have the tags still on them.

They arrived at an office building. It was only as they were going up in an elevator from the parking garage that Sasha had the opportunity to

whisper to Alice, "Blagodatnoye." One of the guards backhanded Sasha, causing a trickle of blood.

"Silence," he ordered. He seemed to enjoy seeing the woman hurt. Sasha glared up at him in defiance. Alice's strange eyes began to change color, but only one person in the elevator noticed, the large Slavic woman, and she thought it a trick of the light.

They got out on the top floor. A gold plate that read Brenhov Компании and Brenhov Kompanii in both Russian and English lettering was on the wall next to an office. Sasha widened her eyes at the sight. She had recognized the building, but didn't realize that anyone other than her staff or Alexis had access. They were ushered right through the mahogany doors and into a spacious office. Sitting behind the desk was the same white-haired man that Alice had observed so long ago back in the library in Vereya. She realized now, with his age and pale albino countenance, he had to be the patriarch of the Baltizar family. He smiled when he saw the two blonde women in handcuffs.

"Ah, Ms. Brenhov," he said charmingly. "Do have a seat," he gestured to the two chairs before the mahogany desk.

Alice looked around…the office was nice. The wood was stained dark and rich and obviously the mahogany theme had been carried throughout the décor. She liked it, finding the wood warm and charming. The atmosphere in the room though was decidedly chilly.

"That's nice of you, considering this is my office," Sasha felt brave enough to answer dryly, as she and Alice took the seats across from the large desk.

He smiled at her and then glanced at the woman escorting them as she handed him the laptop. "Were you able to get into this?" he asked and she shook her head. "No worries, I have people…" he began and then stopped when he saw Alice smile. "Something funny?" he asked.

"No," she answered and smiled fully. She could see it irritated him. His eyes were a pale blue, almost white. It was chilling. She only stopped smiling when he looked back at his people and couldn't see her anymore.

"Unlock them," he ordered, indicating the cuffs.

"Sir, I would suggest…" began the Slavic woman.

"You would what?" he intoned warningly and cut her off.

Quieting, she stood back when the two men leaned over with handcuff keys to unlock the women.

Xander Baltizar began, "Ms. Brenhov, I have a few documents for you to sign…." He would have continued, but was interrupted by the noise coming from his right.

As soon as Alice's hands were released, her fingers poked as hard as they could into the man leaning over her. Her legs intertwined with his and sent him crashing into the man who had unlocked Sasha's wrists a little quicker. Both women scooted out of the way and Alice used her chair to crash into the large Slavic woman's path as she charged at Alice. Next, Alice's hand went to her belt. She saw Sasha note the hand gesture and she and Alice went back to back as Alice threw not one, but three knives in quick order. She didn't stop to watch the effect of her knives…she saw where they hit and watched as the woman paused. Alice then turned, Sasha still at her back, turning with her. She faced the albino man and watched as he reached for a gun. Her throws were off, nicking him, and he got a shot off before she threw another knife and then her own body at him, knocking the gun out of the way as it went off again. Alice's body, while not heavy, startled the older man and he fell back into his chair, dropping the gun. She grabbed one more knife from her belt and held it at his neck.

"Move and I slice it will," she said imperfectly in Russian, but he understood. He *really* understood as he could feel the sharp edge at his neck. He could see the Slav had fallen to the ground, two of these triangular knives in her throat, the third grotesquely in her forehead. His arms reached out to the sides, straight out, to show he had nothing in them. Alice slowly got up off the chair they had both slammed back into. "Sasha, bring those cuffs," she ordered. When she wasn't immediately answered, she glanced over to see Sasha was down on the ground. Whether wounded or hiding, she wasn't sure as the desk was blocking her view. Just the glance away had her captive bringing down his arms and she stabbed him just a little to get his attention again. The trickle of blood did the job. "Uh uh, move without permission again…" she warned. She moved around behind him, her back to the large window as she surveyed the room. She slowly moved him and the chair that was on rollers around the edge of the desk, her hand at his neck with the sharp knife pricking him.

As Alice came around the first corner she could see Sasha was down and out, again she wasn't sure if she was hurt. The man saw it too and at the angle he was to her, she could see satisfaction in his eyes. For a second, Alice wondered if he saw something she didn't. "Get on your knees and hands," she ordered him.

Incredulous, he tried to look up at her. She obviously didn't know the price of the suit he was wearing. Alice pulled the knife away slightly so he could move, her other hand no longer pushing the chair, but his shoulder. He looked up and nearly gasped. Used to his own unusually pale blue eyes, now he saw yellow eyes and hers appeared to be like a cat. They were a deep gold right now and an impossible shade of orange. He had never seen anything like it. Her shove sent him to the floor on his knees. He mentally cursed at her for the damage to his suit and the pain to his old

body. The knife was back at his neck, right by the artery, and he put his hands down.

"Bring me those handcuffs." She could see the guard that had lost his eyesight—she knew how deeply her fingers had thrust—was holding his face with his hands, sobbing. The other guard was slowly getting up and it looked like he was reaching for something. "Uh uh, handcuffs or he dies," she thrust a little again, causing more blood to trickle into the white of his suit shirt.

"Get the handcuffs!" the older man ordered his guard. Inwardly he was cursing his people for their stupidity. These three should have been able to handle the two women!

Alice had the guard handcuff the albino man face down on the carpet with his hands behind his back. She knew at his age he would not be able to get up too fast and cause trouble. Next, she had the guard handcuff himself on one wrist and she handcuffed the other, again behind the man, while he lay on the ground.

"You bitch! What did you do to me?" the other guard whined.

"Shut up! You knew the risks working this man for," she told him imperfectly. "I could just kill you," she offered conversationally. He quieted after that, only pain-filled breaths told of his injury. She checked on Sasha next and glanced at the Slav. She wasn't breathing, but Sasha was. Alice found a bullet hole in her arm. As she rolled her friend over, she heard her moan.

"Alice?" she asked, groggily.

"You fainted," she teased her.

"What? I never..." she began and then groaned at the pain in her arm. "He shot me!" she gasped, shocked.

"Yes, he did. Good thing you moving were or you'd dead be," Alice told her with a smile.

Sasha looked around the room and, seeing the others, wondered what she had missed. Alice was definitely efficient...perhaps too efficient. Not something she hadn't thought of before. Right now though, her concern was for her arm. She looked down as Alice began to pull her jacket off. She hissed at the pain in her arm.

"Sorry," Alice offered weakly. She looked through the shirt and ripped it away from where the bullet had gone in. "I think I'm going to have to take this out."

"We should go to the hospital–" Sasha began and then realized how stupid that sounded as Alice cut her off.

"And risk questions?" Her eyebrow being raised over one eye was enough to make Sasha squirm.

Nodding, the platinum blonde agreed with Alice...whatever she wanted to do.

"Here, get in a chair." Alice helped her get up and straightened one of the chairs. "I told you not to move," she yelled at the albino and kicked him for good measure. "Do it again and you won't like the consequences," she promised.

"I'd believe her, Xander," Sasha said to him. "She helped me kill two of your sons." She felt no remorse for telling him that. Normally those cold eyes of his would have had her shuddering. She remembered how angry he had been when he informed her she would marry one of his sons. At that time, she had felt young and helpless. Now she felt it was time for payback.

"You? You killed my boys?" he gasped incredulously. "You don't have it in you!"

"I've changed, Xander. You and your ilk forced me to. You and your precious Assemblage."

"You were offered a chance to join..." he began defensively.

"I made more without you all!"

"We made more without you around," he laughed.

"Not anymore," Alice put in with a look at him. "I'd shut up for now if I were you," she told him and the look in her odd yellow-orange eyes told him to be quiet for now. Alice turned back to Sasha, "You ready for this?" she indicated the torn shirt and the hole that was bubbling blood.

"Yeah, you better find a needle and thread...there's alcohol over there," she indicated a large globe of the world and watched as Alice opened it to find alcohol. One by one, Alice looked over the expensive bottles of various liquors and fine drinks. She chose one and brought it back.

"Got any needles or thread?"

"Actually, in the drawer over there," she indicated the wall of bookshelves with drawers in the bottom half. "Second from the bottom."

Alice found a sewing kit and looked at Sasha in surprise.

"What am I to do?" whined the guard who was holding his hands to his now sightless eyes.

Alice looked again at Sasha who looked disgustedly at the man. At Alice's look, she tilted her head sideways and shrugged. Alice nodded, stepped to the man, and slit his throat. His gurgling only lasted a little while before he bled out.

"You can't..." began the other guard, but a well-aimed kick of Alice's had him shutting up.

"We can and we will. Neither of two you deserve more," she tried to tell them.

"Neither of you two," Sasha corrected without thinking.

Alice looked again at the platinum blonde and Sasha explained. She laughed at her mistakes, but she was improving.

"This is going to hurt," she warned.

"Just do it!"

Sasha watched as Alice retrieved the various blades she had thrown, some of them quite bloody, and placed them on the edge of the desk. She looked for and found a lighter. Heating one of the 'clean' blades after she washed it in alcohol, they both watched as it flamed up for a moment, eating at the alcohol.

"Both you stay still or this goes you in next," Alice warned the two men laying on their stomachs. She knew she would be concentrating on Sasha and it would be a good time for either of them to cause her trouble or attack.

Once the blade was cleaned by the alcohol and warmed by the lighter, Alice wiped it and then began to gently probe in Sasha's arm. The blade was too wide and she worried she would cause more damage. "I have to find something else to take this out."

"Look on that shelf, there is a probe of sorts for slicing off gold," Sasha said, nodding towards the glassed-in shelves.

Alice walked over her captives, hopped really, and went to the shelving units. "Do you have a key?" she asked as she tried the door.

"I don't know where it would be," Sasha admitted. She'd been here a few times of course, but she didn't work here. That's why she had general managers. She wondered where he was at the moment, or his secretary that should have been in the outer office.

Alice didn't hesitate. Sasha had been bleeding for too long and she needed to get that bullet out. Using a quick elbow thrust, she hoped her jacket would protect her skin. The shattering glass had everyone in the

room jumping. She immediately reached for the small pinchers. They would be much better than the probe. She hurried back to her patient, hopping over the two bodies on the floor and walking around the one bleeding out. His body released a bunch of pent up gas, loudly, and Alice wrinkled her nose distastefully at the sound.

"Let's get this cleaned up," she said to Sasha in English. She showed her the pinchers and quickly cleaned them with alcohol.

She approached Sasha and pulled up on her arm slightly to get a better angle. She quickly probed inside with the pincher, feeling for the bullet.

"Holy SHIT! That HURTS!" her English was noticeably clear on that phrase.

Alice felt resistance and opened the pinchers slightly. She felt the hardness of the bullet, but it slipped away due to the blood. She pushed harder, causing Sasha more pain. She sensed the platinum blonde looking up at her in alarm. She almost had the bullet when she sensed, rather than heard, the guard move.

"Oh, no, you don't," she said, pulling the pinchers out just in time as he rushed her. He had managed to get to his feet and was using a football charge to try to knock her off her feet. Alice side-stepped just in time, pushing against his body momentum to have him go crashing into the book shelves behind her. She followed through, dropping the pinchers and pulling one of her belt knives. She didn't hesitate as she used his crash and momentary confusion to slit his throat. His gurgling could be heard by them all as he turned to stare up at her in horror, his arms behind him in the cuffs. He choked on his own blood before he died.

"Now, you," she said pointing to the albino who was staring at her, wondering at how cold-blooded the woman was. "Stay put or I'll gut you from naval to neck," she tried to translate the saying imperfectly. "If you

want to live, cooperate you!" she warned. She put the bloody little triangle on the desk with the others.

"Let's finish this," she said to Sasha and bent to retrieve the pinchers. They seemed a little bent and she hid that from Sasha so she could clean them once again with the alcohol. She poured extra out onto the various blades sitting in a pile on the desk. She turned back to Sasha to begin her attempt to pull out the bullet. "I'm sorry," she said in English in advance of the hurt she was going to cause her. "You want a drink?" she offered, but Sasha shook her head, gritting her teeth.

Sasha was sweating. She thought of the American saying, 'Sweating bullets,' and now understood it better. She was in so much pain and the loss of blood was making her lightheaded. She passed out before Alice finished, slumping forward, causing a tear in the hole that Alice was probing the pinchers in.

"Dammit," Alice swore, but she had gotten a hold of the slippery bullet and wasn't about to let go. Slowly and steadily she pulled it out through the blood. She almost lost it several times, but trying to prop up Sasha and pull it out created a tension she wasn't even aware of. She had to also concentrate on Xander Baltizar and his stealthy movements. "You wish die to, Mr. Baltizar?" she asked him conversationally, never taking her eyes off the pinchers. She heard no more movement. When she finally had the bullet out, she let Sasha slump to the ground. She couldn't hold her up anymore. Gently she eased her down, grabbed the bottle, and poured it over the wound. She probed once more with the bent pinchers and pulled out the cloth of the blouse that Sasha had been wearing. She poured more alcohol in the wound. She felt her hands shaking as she tried to thread a needle. She had to use a little contraption that allowed her to push it through the eye of the needle and then pulled the thread through for her. Biting off a length she knotted it and then poured more liquor on the

bleeding wound and the thread and needle, hoping it was adequate, before efficiently sewing it up. She used tiny stiches, knowing it would scar. She was still shaking and it made it difficult, but she got it done. She was sweating when she was done.

Alice walked over to the second guard she had killed. She removed his handcuffs with the key the other had dropped when she gouged out his eyes and tripped him. Taking the handcuffs, she measured and then cuffed Xander Baltizar's thin ankles together.

"Why?" he huffed, unused to being on his stomach like this for so long.

"Because I trust you can't," she told him.

"Ah, you Americans, can't even learn to speak Russian correctly," he insulted her.

"Ah, you Russians, can't even learn to fight properly," she told him in return. This time she got her syntax correct, but didn't even know it since Sasha wasn't awake to correct her. She looked over at her friend and then went to her, pulling her to the couch in the office by the door and hoisting her on to it. Her limp body was so relaxed Alice worried she had died for a moment and was relieved to see her breathing. She looked around and went through some drawers before she found a blanket to put on her, covering her up and warming her. She looked around the office, wondering if she should clean it up or wait. She saw a small bathroom in the corner she hadn't noticed before and wondered why she hadn't. Then she saw that it had one of those pressure doors that aligned with the shelving units, the guard must have crashed into it to make it swing open. She went in to wash her hands.

"Could I have a drink of water?" the Russian called.

Alice prepared two cups from the cooler in the corner, one for when Sasha woke up and one for the older Russian. She carefully poured it for

him. "Turn head so don't choke," she advised as she slowly helped him to drink. She wouldn't touch him, but poured slowly so he could gulp it down. "Now answer questions for me," she advised.

"What would you like to know?" he asked, considering what he could tell the American.

"Why did you me take?"

"You were an accident," he confirmed Alice's suspicions. He told her that their hirelings hadn't known which woman was Sasha Brenhov and as a result, she was taken too. By the time they realized their mistake, it was too late. "How did you escape?" he asked. They hadn't gotten the complete details they wanted from their people.

Alice didn't answer him. She was going to be the one to ask the questions. She saw that Sasha was beginning to stir and went over to her friend, brushing her long hair back from her face. "Hey, you okay?" she asked kindly in English.

"Vhat…?" Sasha answered back. She tried to sit up, then remembered her arm due to the pain and looked down. "Did you…?"

"I got it," Alice told her. It was clean now and no blood seeping out. "Let me bandage that and keep it clean," she offered.

"You love her?" Baltizar asked from across the room where he was watching the two women. He knew from his sons that Brenhov was a dyke. He hadn't known this Weaver woman was one too.

Alice turned her eyes on him; they began to change color as he watched. "I'll have you know, bastard you, that she is friend my," she said with a tone in her voice that made him and Sasha distinctly uncomfortable. He was mesmerized by her cat-like eyes. They were turning that odd orange-yellow combination again.

"Alice," Sasha warned weakly in English. "It's not worth it."

"Have him answer my questions. Translate for me, please?" Alice asked her.

Sasha nodded and Alice got up to go to the laptop they had placed on the desk. She opened it and found an internet signal. She had Sasha begin to ask Baltizar questions about what he had purchased of the Brenhov holdings. When he went silent and refused to answer, Alice calmly got up and began to kick him. Leaning over him, she pulled one of her knives— she was running out of them—and calmly told him in Russian, "Answer our questions or I will peel face off." He believed her.

One by one, and it took a long time, Alice got her questions answered. She pulled up financial records she hadn't known existed and it made it easier. She only had to get up once and start for the older man to get him to babble out everything she wanted. She knew he wasn't telling them everything, especially the account numbers that were consistently off by one number. Her programs helped her with passwords too and she said nothing to indicate that she knew he was lying. He told her enough that he thought he was getting away with something. Alice found more than he intended. She also knew there was a lot more to research with what she had found by interrogating him.

Finally, Sasha was exhausted. The loss of blood, the stress, everything was catching up with her. Their prisoner was exhausted as well. Alice had enough that she began to transfer funds from Xander Baltizar's accounts, both personal and professional. She shocked him twice when she asked him for the passwords to get through some of the safety features he had installed, much less that she had found them. He knew she was clever, but he hadn't thought she was *that* clever.

"You realize my other sons will avenge what has been done to me and my boys," he warned Sasha.

"Have they found your boys?" she asked with deadly accuracy.

He deflated at that taunt. Alice watched as he visibly aged before them. She knew it was time to pack it up.

Sasha sat up as Alice closed the laptop. She saw that Alice had backed it all up on the small flash drive she carried in her pocket, but knew that Xander had not. Even though they had gotten the laptop, they couldn't have gotten into it. Alice had taught Sasha how to encrypt the password so that only they could get into it. Alice put the flash drive back into her pocket.

"Are you up for an adventure?" Alice asked her friend.

"I'm not," she admitted wearily.

"Is there somewhere we can sleep here?"

"There is an apartment upstairs."

Alice nodded, not surprised. A gold mine must be hell to stay at. "Where the hell is your general manager?"

Sasha asked Baltizar, who admitted that they had killed the man and his secretary.

"Where are the bodies?" Alice asked.

"Shaft 129."

Sasha was horrified, but this just gave Alice an idea.

Alice left Baltizar in the office while she helped Sasha into the elevator and they rode to the top floor. The apartment was sparse, but functional. Alice found soup and other things in the small captain's kitchen. She made some for her friend, adding plenty of salt to help her blood, and gave her a bowl with crackers. She also drank a cup of it, but she wasn't that hungry. She had work to do and was anxious to start. Alice gave Sasha a washcloth to wipe down the sweat from her forehead as she helped her to the bathroom, turning aside while she did what she had to do. She tucked her in one of the two bedrooms and told her she'd be back. Sasha didn't

notice much. She was too tired and the hot food had made her sleepy. She was asleep before the elevator arrived to take Alice to the floor below.

Alice looked in on Baltizar, and saw that he was in a considerable amount of pain lying on his stomach with the handcuffs holding his hands behind his back and encasing his ankles. He had obviously tried to move, but his age and the restraints were against him. Alice left him to go search the building for more. She was surprised she encountered no one: no guards, no employees. She'd have to ask Baltizar about that later. She too was tired. It had been a long day. She wanted to finish her 'work' and finish it now.

Alice found a platform dolly in what must be the building's shipping and receiving department. She maneuvered it into the elevator and went back up to the office of the general manager. Slowly, with much effort, she lifted the Slav woman onto it. The woman was huge, bigger actually than the two guards. Next, Alice had to get one and then the other guard onto the dolly too. Stacking them didn't work too well. Their bodies had begun to stiffen in the hours since she had killed them. She managed to get them on the rolling cart and into the elevator. She heard Baltizar trying to yell at her, but the water she had given him certainly wasn't enough to keep him hydrated. She'd let him suffer some more. No one was in the building to hear him.

Alice went down the ramp by the shipping and receiving. She looked for and found a truck open at the back. The cart rolled right in, just in time for one of the guards to fall off of it for the last time. She left him on the floor of the truck, closed the roll-up door, and looked for the keys…she found them in the visor. She then began to ease the truck out of the bay where it had been parked. The cold was taking her breath away this late at night. She followed the lights to what she had to assume was the mine.

She was relieved to pass through a checkpoint, waved through by the two guards. She hadn't known if she would have to fight her way in, but they obviously recognized the truck. Alice looked for and found markers of some sort. Most were in Russian, but a few also had English on them. It took a while, a lot of driving around, before she came across what must be Shaft 129. She backed the truck up to it, hitting the back of the truck against the dirt. She set the parking brake and got out. Stretching, she realized she was exhausted now. She was a petite woman and the stress she had in her body was wearing on it. Still, she carried on. The second guard's body had rolled off the cart. Alice didn't care. She pulled and pushed and got the cart off the truck, leaving the two dead guards as she headed into Shaft 129. There were lights on, but they were dimmed this late at night. She almost fell into the actual shaft as she tried to get the rolling cart across the hard, packed dirt. She pushed and shoved and grunted and groaned until she got the Slav to the side of the hole. She pushed her over the edge and then one by one went back for the guards. The shaft must be very deep, she never heard the bodies hit the bottom. It was quite late before she finished, threw the dolly in the truck, and headed back to the office building. She tried to remember where to park the truck and leave the keys. She even put the dolly back, looking regretfully at the blood on the bottom of the truck and on the dolly. There was nothing she could do about that now, and really, what would it matter?

Alice returned to the office. Baltizar wasn't even coherent. He was in a lot of pain, but Alice just looked at him a moment before she retrieved her laptop and put it in its bag. She ignored his pleas as she headed back to the elevator, avoiding the blood stains on the carpet. Alice finally got a shower in the early morning hours, a hot one, as hot as she could stand. She found some odd clothing in a drawer and pulled it on. It fit improperly and reminded her of something you would find in a doctor's

office. Her clothes were officially ruined. She remembered her new clothes were still in the car downstairs and wondered where the driver had gone with them…had he gone somewhere? She hadn't looked for the limo. She'd worry about it tomorrow. She was too tired now and she needed some sleep.

~ ~ ~ ~ ~

Alice woke slowly to sunshine in her eyes. The glare of it had her blinking rapidly.

"Hey, you're awake," Sasha said as she stuck her head in the doorway.

"Barely," Alice grumbled.

"It's noon," she was informed.

Alice nodded and stretched. She hadn't gotten to bed until the early morning hours. Sleeping in was a luxury she had enjoyed in Dubai, she'd miss it now. "How are you feeling?"

"Better with a meal under my belt."

Alice realized they were speaking Russian. The translations were never perfect and made her laugh. She knew she would never 'master' this language, but thought she was doing better after all this time.

"What are we doing today?" Sasha asked, noticing the weird clothes Alice had on.

"We should find out about going back to the plane if we can," Sasha informed her as she stretched again. A terrific yawn practically split her face in two. She ran her hand through her short, spikey hair. She was kind of liking it this short now.

"Where is Xander?" she hesitated to ask.

"Oh shit, I left him in the office," Alice told her.

"He's going to be angry."

"He might have died, for all I care." Alice got up from the bed, feeling every bit of the previous long night and those heavy bodies.

"Are we going to kill him?"

"Do you want to?"

"I don't think we have a choice."

Alice agreed and then dismissed it. She was hungry and she needed to pee. Within half an hour she had taken care of both problems. "I have to find clothes," she told Sasha as she looked down at the odd smock and balloon pants she was wearing. They were a godawful powder blue too.

"Do you think the car is still downstairs?"

"I have no idea, but could you check? If the driver is still around..." she warned.

"I'll look," she volunteered and headed for the elevator.

Alice looked out at the view. The office building wasn't that tall, but it was the tallest building around and had an unobstructed view of the mine, or rather the mines. There were diggings all along this section of the river. She saw a tent city of some sort down a ways and could see people there...she wondered at that.

Sasha returned, lugging the larger of Alice's two suitcases. Alice was relieved to get into designer blue jeans and a sweatshirt that read 'Dubai' on it, showing the silhouette of the city in the desert by the sea. She was glad to get into clean underwear and change into her boots—she was able to put a knife in the scabbard of her boot and place her jeans over them. She finger-combed her hair and felt 'dressed.' For the first time in a long time, she wished she could put on makeup and thought it odd that she would think of that at a time like this.

"What should I do with these?" Sasha asked as she saw Alice's blood and muck-covered clothes.

"Burn them," Alice answered, short and sweet.

Sasha understood. They were a mess, but not much more so than when they were on that farm weeks ago. Was it only weeks ago? It seemed so much longer. She rolled them up and put them in a plastic bag for the maid to throw out, thought better of it, and dragged it into the elevator. They left the bag and Alice's suitcase in the outer office as they went to go check on Baltizar.

He was barely conscious. Alice went and got him a cup of water and sprinkled it on his face as she wet his tongue. She knew he wouldn't be able to walk after a night in that cramped position and she unlocked the cuffs on his legs.

"Watch him," she warned Sasha as she went back to the elevator.

"Where are you going?"

"To get something to help us." She pulled the bag containing her soiled clothes into the elevator with her when it arrived and pressed the ground floor button. She knew her way to the shipping and receiving area well now. She threw the bag into a dumpster and found a clean platform dolly. She noticed a couple of Jeeps and Humvees as well as Russian versions of the same type of vehicle with the Brenhov logo on them and filed that away in her agile mind. She quickly returned upstairs with the dolly.

"Help me get him onto this," she told Sasha.

Between the two of them, they heaved the older man onto the dolly. He looked bad, very bad, from his night in cuffs. Alice didn't remove them from his wrists. She wheeled the dolly back into the elevator and they all took a ride, Sasha bringing her suitcase along for her.

"I'll meet you out front," she promised Sasha, who looked at her curiously. Alice headed for the rear of the building, now very familiar

with shipping and receiving. She confiscated one of the Jeeps, finding the key in the ignition. Now that Baltizar's legs were functioning again, they got him inside, in the back. At first he refused, but she conversationally threatened him and he complied. Living was always worth the effort.

"Where did you find this?" Sasha said with a laugh as she got in. She knew, but she was feeling better. The Assemblage hadn't gotten this property. She still owned it, at least she hoped she did. "Where do you want to go?" she asked Alice as she began to drive.

"Do you think he speaks English?" Alice asked, nodding towards the back seat where Baltizar lay.

"Probably," Sasha answered, "he's a crafty old bird."

"You could have been great, the children you would have had," he rasped from the back in Russian.

"Shut up, you old devil," she shot back. He quieted, but only because he was too tired…that water hadn't been enough. He wondered what they had in mind for him.

Alice drove towards the tent city she had seen from above. As she got closer, she saw that people were living in it despite the severe cold. There were shacks too and it looked like a shanty town. "What is this?" she asked, alarmed.

"I have no idea," Sasha admitted. "It was not here the last time I visited."

"How long ago was that?"

"Years."

Alice looked around and was disgusted by the conditions.

"Hold up, I see one of the managers. I remember him."

Alice slowed the Jeep, downshifting.

In rapid Russian, Sasha called to the man.

"Ms. Brenhov," he saluted her, surprised. "It has been a long time."

"Vitaly, isn't it?"

He was pleased she remembered his name and smiled at her. "Yes, ma'am."

"What has happened here? What is this place?"

He lost his smile. "Your manager set this up. He thought the men needed 'entertainment.'"

Sasha looked around, saw that Alice had understood too, and listened as the man continued.

"Eventually they didn't bother to go back to town, but many stayed here and live here now."

"There are women?" Alice asked, frostily.

He leaned forward looking at the driver, noticing the American accent. He glanced in the back and saw Baltizar. He looked surprised at the man lying there. He looked back at the owner of the mine. Gulping, he answered with a nod. "Yes, there are women here."

Alice exchanged a look with Sasha who nodded knowingly. They both wondered if some of these women were from the farm, or had Sasha's manager been corrupted by The Assemblage.

"Tell the men to get back to work…" Sasha began.

"I haven't seen the general manager…" he began to protest. "It's Sunday," he finished lamely.

"I don't care if it is Sunday. Those men are to start tearing down those tents and shanties by the time I return or I'll burn them," Sasha promised.

The man gulped and nodded, this was the owner he remembered.

"I'll be back soon."

With that, Alice released the clutch and they lurched away. It had been a while since she drove a manual versus an automatic and it took some finagling as she shifted from one gear to the next.

"Do you think my manager...?" Sasha asked in English in the hopes that Baltizar didn't understand them.

"Probably, but we both know who is ultimately to blame," Alice finished for her, also in English.

"Vhere are ve going?"

"Do you know how far these plains go?" she indicated the track that was taking them out onto the plains. They were past the river and heading out into the great nothing.

"For many miles," she admitted.

"We'll drop him out there," Alice commented.

Sasha couldn't think of a more fitting end for the man in the back seat. She was done feeling guilty for killing anyone in The Assemblage. Her arm was killing her. Her girlfriend had been beaten. The money, well that could be replaced. In fact, from the transfers Alice had made for them, even splitting it, she stood to make a profit.

~ ~ ~ ~ ~

It was years later before someone found a Russian body in the permafrost in a remote area of the country near a goldmine. He was later identified as prominent Russian businessman Xander Baltizar, but only after a DNA test was run on the frozen body. He had been reported missing by his wife, but no one had any idea where he had gone. Oddly, he had handcuffs on his wrists. It had been widely believed that he had taken money from his connections and hidden away somewhere in the world. It was unknown where that particular rumor had started.

~ ~ ~ ~ ~

Alice and Sasha returned to find most of the tent city dismantled. The men had simply shoved the prostitutes out on their own, with the little clothing that they had. The women were milling about in the cold, unsure of what to do.

Alice was immediately and fully angry! Those men had used the women while they had their uses, probably abused them too. She wondered how many of them were willing in the first place.

"Come," she called, willing to take them in the Jeep. They looked at each other in wonderment...should they go with the strange woman? "Tell them to come with us. We'll get them back to their homes or civilization," Alice told Sasha.

Sasha, her accent untainted, told them exactly that. Only three could fit in the back of the Jeep.

"We will be back for the you rest of," Alice promised. They exchanged looks until another woman called to Alice in English.

"Are you American?"

"Yes, I am," Alice told her, surprised to hear a southern accent coming from the badly made-up prostitute.

"I'm from Georgia," she told her excitedly.

"I'm from California," Alice answered. "You tell those girls I'll be back for the rest of you," she looked around at the dozen women, wondering how many men they had to service in a day.

The Georgia peach began babbling excitedly in Russian to the other women as Alice popped the clutch and began driving away. The three women in the back were shivering from the cold because the heat in the Jeep wasn't that high. Alice drove right up to the limousine and got out.

"Did you happen to see the driver?" she asked Sasha.

"No, I never did. I bet he was down there," she nodded towards the tent town still visible as the men continued to pull it down.

Alice climbed into the limousine and found the keys. Why these people always put them in the visor she didn't know, but it worked in her favor. "Get them in the back. We'll go get the others," she told Sasha. She watched as Sasha helped the women out and got in the back with them. Alice slowly drove away from the office building and back to the tent city.

The women were excited to be riding in a limousine. They barely fit in the back, some sitting on the laps of others. Sasha sat up front with Alice and they rolled down the little window between the front and the back.

"Where are we going?" the woman from Georgia asked.

"We're going to try to catch a plane," Alice promised.

Sasha exchanged a glance with Alice and pointed out some of the directions she remembered from her last trip there.

"Oh, damn!" Alice exclaimed as they made their way onto the airport grounds and headed for the only plane there.

"Vhat?" Sasha looked around, worried that Alice had seen something she hadn't.

"I forgot my links," she indicated the knives that made up her belt.

"You vant to go back for them?" she joked.

Alice laughed and shook her head. She was already planning ahead to what they would do about the pilot.

They got the women out of the warm limousine and into the cold plane. It hadn't been readied for them, but then no one knew they were coming. Alice got their luggage on the plane, handing it to Sasha who took it in. The private plane was crowded with the dozen prostitutes, but they weren't going to leave any of the women behind. The woman from Georgia had

confirmed what they both suspected, none of the women were there voluntarily, but none knew how to escape or even where they were really.

Alice had just finished handing their laptop bag up to Sasha when two men came hurrying up. Alice had pulled her nail gun out of one of their bags and hoped the battery still held a charge. She pointed it at the captain. "You for the Beltizars work?"

He shook his head, trying to understand the woman. Sasha repeated it for him clearly.

"I work for The Assemblage," he told her proudly.

"Now you work for me," Sasha told him imperiously, knowing how best to work with these kind of employees after years of practice.

"Who are you?" he asked, annoyed at the odd gun being pointed at him. The blonde woman holding it had strange eyes.

"I am Sasha Brenhov," she informed him, her tone changing to one of command. "If you wish to retain your job, you will get paid well."

"And her?" he thumbed at Alice holding the gun.

"She'll shoot you if you don't."

"How do you know that I won't bail in the sky?" he asked.

"How do you know I won't shoot this through your skull?" Alice asked in halting Russian. It was obvious that she didn't speak it well. It didn't mean she didn't understand it.

He looked at the odd gun, realized it shot nails, and gulped at the pain that would cause. Trying to brave it out he looked back at the platinum blonde. He knew who she was. "How do I know you will pay me?"

She stared him down and finally he nodded. He and his co-pilot entered the plane and began their pre-flight checklist. Alice followed them, not only to get away from the chattering women in the cabin, but to watch him and make him a bit nervous. She kept the safety trigger under

her thumb, one quick slide and she could trigger a nail quickly into her intended victim. She hoped she wouldn't have to.

They were soon in the sky; the plane had been gassed up as soon as it landed. Alice had told him to plan to go back to the exact airport they had left in Moscow. She sat there the entire flight and watched them both. She didn't answer any of the questions they asked her over the long flight, instead she stared at them with her oddly unblinking eyes. She waited until they turned around again to quickly blink back the tears caused by trying not to blink.

It seemed to take forever for them to get clearance to land. Alice listened closely in case they tried anything funny. She wasn't sure if it was the promise of Sasha's money or the nail gun she held that kept them honest, but they landed safely. Sasha went into the airport to arrange a bus to pick up all of their passengers. The women kept thanking Alice and she had to wonder what Sasha had told them about her.

~ ~ ~ ~ ~

Trying to arrange identification and passports for these women was a nightmare. Yuri Azarov was a big help, but as he said, he knew people. He got paid well for the service too. He had been shocked when over a dozen women got off the train in Vologda where Sasha had called and arranged for them to meet. She paid cash, and she paid well. She'd given the pilots more than double their fee and promised them more if they worked for her and not The Assemblage. She stressed that keeping their mouths shut would ensure their safety and lives.

Yuri had to travel all the way from Vereya to Vologda and she made it worth his while. Getting passports for the Russian and other European

women was fairly easy, it was the foreign ones, like the American from Georgia, that were proving difficult.

"Come on, Yuri," Sasha said exasperatedly. "You can do this!"

"You don't understand. The United States has made it harder to fake these," he protested.

Alice and Sasha both knew he was lying, since each of them had at least three fake ones of their own. Sasha could see Alice was becoming angry at his delays. There was something...suddenly Alice pulled out her boot knife and held it up to Yuri's neck.

"You sold us out, didn't you?" she asked him conversationally. Her knee came up and held him in the chair he was sitting in.

He immediately broke out in a sweat. He put his hands out at his sides to show he wasn't going to fight her. He would have shaken his head, but that would have given him a helluva cut across his neck. "N...no...I wouldn't. I didn't," he stuttered, alarmed.

"Then why the American can't you a passport get?" Alice asked, imperfectly.

"I can!" he insisted. "I will!"

"Alice," Sasha said warningly. They needed Yuri and his connections.

"You better," Alice told the man, looking deeply into his fear-filled eyes.

Yuri didn't know if he was more afraid of the knife or the odd-colored eyes as they changed before him. He knew he couldn't, wouldn't, screw over this woman. She would hunt him down if it took the rest of her life...and it would his. He swallowed reflexively, and once she pulled the knife away, nodded in agreement.

All of the women had been photographed, given money, and a plane ticket to the country of their choice. Some chose to go home; others chose

to move on. Some would return to the life they had just left; others would start over. All they had left was the American.

"Honey, I need to get out of here," she said fearfully. She was certain someone would come for her, come for *them*. It had taken so much time to arrange everything.

"We've got you covered," Alice assured her. The woman was getting on her nerves with her sickeningly-sweet southern accent. She wasn't sure if it was the woman herself or Alice's hormones. Her period had come on and it was making her very irritable.

When the woman was in the other hotel room they had rented, Alice turned to Sasha. "We need to go to Switzerland," she told her.

"Vhy?" Sasha asked. They were speaking English, probably because Yuri could hear them. Even then they weren't so sure he couldn't understand them.

"I'll tell you later," Alice assured her, glancing at the man making his phone calls to get the documents for the American woman to travel. She wanted the woman to travel with them to Switzerland. Three women traveling together wouldn't be as noticeable, especially when they were looking for the two of them.

"I'm going to check something," Alice said to Sasha meaningfully, glancing at Yuri to tell Sasha, without saying anything, to keep an eye on the guy. He had a few more hours to come up with the paperwork he had promised.

Alice took their car, which they had retrieved. She'd decided to sell it as she didn't want it tracked back to them. She took the bus after selling it on one of the more affluent streets and began to walk down the street in broad daylight. The address she had gotten from one of her computer runs brought her to a slightly run-down Georgian mansion. Looking around carefully, she was up and over the wrought iron fence before anyone really

saw her. She made her way to the front door, noticing that while the driveway was swept of snow, the rest of the place was sadly neglected. In no time at all she was inside and looking around. There was no one here, but it was obvious someone lived here occasionally.

She went through the entire house: the eight bedrooms, the two living rooms, even the six bathrooms. The library was beautiful, but missing all of its books. She wondered at this as well as the lack of security. The house was heated, barely, and she kept her outside clothes on. The gloves had an added bonus of her not leaving fingerprints. As a matter of course, she put a keylogger and worm program on the computer she found. Other than that, she felt the trip was a bust...and then she found the safe. It was behind one of the painted pictures, showing a scene of St. Petersburg that must be from colonial times. Normally she had left the safes alone in the various homes she had been in that belonged to members of The Assemblage, but on this occasion, she felt she had the time. Using a small suction cupped device, she was able to play with the dial until she heard the satisfying clicks that indicated she had hit the right numbers. Inside she found various deeds and paperwork, some of which she could actually read since it wasn't all in Russian. Those she couldn't read, she took pictures of with her phone, so that Sasha could help her later to interpret them. She carefully returned them to the safe, in the same order she had taken them out so as not to arouse suspicion...in case anyone else was as detail-oriented as Alice was.

Alice took one more look around the house before she let herself out. The house had been used, but it wasn't lived in, and that bothered her for some reason. She made her way down the drive and was out and over the gate with no one really noticing her...or so she thought. She made her way to the bus line and got lost in the crowds, taking an extra bus to shake

any would-be followers. It was a good thing she did, as she had picked up a tail. They lost her in the crowds and with the extra bus trick. She returned to their hotel.

"Does he got them?" she indicated Yuri and the paperwork.

"Just," Sasha assured her, wondering where Alice had been all this time.

"Let me see," Alice commanded, peeling off her winter clothing. It had been cold outside. She left on her gloves so as not to touch the paperwork. Slowly, one by one, she looked at the passport and other paperwork for the American woman. Her eye noted that it was a forgery, but most wouldn't be quite as critical as she. It also had a few fake stamps on the passport, proving the woman had entered Russia 'legally.' "Nice touch," she told Yuri as she examined the stamps.

He nodded in reply. He hoped his work for her was done. He wanted to take his money and leave. He hoped never to have anything to do with her again. She made him far too nervous.

"By the way, those two men who hassled you a while back?" At his nod, she continued, "They won't ever hassle you again." She said it with such conviction and certainty that he believed her. Those men had to be dead.

He was ever so relieved when she informed him that 'he could go.' Gathering his things, he waited while Sasha handed him an envelope full of his payment for his work and connections. He was relieved by that too as he had used their other payments to pay for this work and was running low. He practically sprinted to get out of their room.

"Let's pack," Alice told Sasha as soon as he was gone. She wasn't certain he wouldn't turn them in and she wanted to get out of here while she could. She went to the door between their suite and the American's and repeated her command. The three of them checked out of the hotel

and headed for the airport to catch a late-night flight to Zurich. From there, the Georgia peach headed on to America with a heartfelt thank you and a bit of cash to tide her over.

"You've been very quiet," Sasha told Alice in French once they were finally alone. It had been a long flight and she was very tired. She was also becoming very nervous by Alice's continued silence.

"I've been thinking," Alice told her unnecessarily.

Sasha waited quietly, hoping Alice would share. She had started to drift to sleep when the other woman spoke again.

"I have photos for you to look at and interpret for us tomorrow while I go to the bank," Alice informed her.

"Bank?" Sasha perked up to fend off her yawn of sleepiness.

"Yes, remember Vashti had a key to a vault here in Switzerland?"

"Yes, I remember."

"I identified it as one of the banks I used to use. I'm hoping that their security precautions are the same and I can still enter as Alice Weaver. If I can get in the vault, they will leave me alone and I can get into Vashti's box. I'll see what I can find. I knew that key looked familiar," she explained.

Sasha thought over how clever this woman had been. Without her and her actions, Sasha wouldn't have been able to get her fortune back, much less take revenge on her enemies. It was going to be much harder to find them from now on. They'd all be scattered.

~ ~ ~ ~ ~

Alice walked into the bank in one of the many outfits she had purchased in Dubai. She looked sharp and she knew it. Her confidence

level was high. Her haughtiness was reminiscent of the days when Alice Weaver was at her height of business transactions. Inside she wasn't feeling that confident, but she knew that looking the part was every bit as important as feeling it. She could bluff her way into the bank—her eye scan, her thumb scan, and she was in. She was taken several flights below the main lobby to the bank of safety deposit boxes. The camera's surveillance stopped at the door. Alice went right to her own vault, using the key the bank had provided for her. As she pushed it in the lock, the bank employee left her alone for privacy's sake. She looked inside, took some of the things she kept there, and put that in her briefcase. She locked the box once again and closed it. Glancing to see if the bank employee was looking in—he wasn't and was far enough away that he couldn't see what she was doing—she looked for and found the box that was Vashti Baltizar's and put in his key. She was pleasantly surprised when it opened. For some reason, she had a moment of worry that the bank had changed something. She couldn't fake being a Baltizar...she couldn't fake being an albino.

Rather than examine the contents, she instead just put them all into her briefcase. At the bottom of the box was a bug, in the shape of an actual bug. She recognized the electronics as something Simone had shown her once while in New York. By hiding a bug within an actual bug, usually live, they could introduce a living bug to someone's apartment and then send an electronic signal to kill the host, allowing them from then on to listen in on whomever they wanted. She wondered why the Baltizars had this in their vault. She wondered if, perhaps, someone who didn't recognize it for what it was would have taken it by accident and been trailed. She left it, and taking the key out, she wiped her fingerprints from it and put the Baltizar key in the box with the bug. Shoving it closed, hard, since the key didn't turn the mechanism, ensured that the key and the bug

were locked inside together. She wiped her fingerprints from the outside of the box too, and taking her briefcase, she left the vault.

"All done?" the bank employee asked her with a smile. It hadn't taken long and he appreciated that. Some customers went through their boxes bit by bit—he was sure counting their millions—and it really took a lot of his time. This woman he'd met once before was always quick and efficient. He wondered what she kept in the box, but of course, he would never ask.

"Yes, thank you," she told him politely in French.

He escorted her upstairs and watched as she put on her expensive and what looked like a tailored coat that their coat check woman helped her with. Alice smiled and tipped the girl as she made her way with her briefcase for the door. Her cat-like eyes were taking in anyone and everyone, in case she recognized someone or they recognized her. She hailed a cab outside and made her way back to the hotel they were staying in.

"Find anything?" Alice asked, as she entered the suite she had rented with Sasha.

"Yes, these people own the deeds to properties scattered throughout Russia, China, Kazakhstan, India, even America," she said pointing at the screen.

Alice got out of her winter clothing, more expensive than what she had worn in Russia. It was colder here in Switzerland right now, but the temps felt different, not as biting. "I got what I went after," she said tapping the briefcase.

"What did you get?" Sasha stretched and got up from where she had been sitting at the laptop too long.

Alice and Sasha spent the day going through the papers that the Baltizars had left in their box. Vashti had paid off many people to hide his indiscretions. Both women wrinkled their noses distastefully at what they read. Sasha was reluctant to translate the Russian items, but did so out of necessity.

The address in Kazakhstan was the same as the one that Alice's phone had taken a picture of, the coincidence couldn't be ignored.

"Are we going to Kazakhstan?" Sasha asked, alarmed.

"We're going to Kazakhstan," Alice confirmed thoughtfully. Some of the paperwork she had found in the safe she now wished she had stolen. The deeds to several important properties were in there. She made a mental note to visit that house once again. Most of Vashti's papers they shredded by hand and threw away, but the few properties they turned over to a lawyer that Alice knew. Strangely, Sasha knew her too.

"We wish to sell these properties," Alice instructed the woman. She left instructions as to how much they would accept, how little she could negotiate to, and forged signatures based on what she had copied from Vashti. Sasha was delighted and amazed.

"And where shall I wire the funds?" the woman inquired loftily. She was used to dealing with such unusual requests. Alice Weaver had given her business from afar many times over the years; however, this was the first time she was dealing with her directly. She had met Sasha Brenhov many times in their dealings. How odd that these two very unlikely women had gone into business together, but she didn't question it.

Alice gave her the information on the accounts where she was to transfer the funds once the properties were sold. She also advised discretion, as she and Sasha both knew The Assemblage had at one time owned these properties. She knew the lawyer handling it out of Switzerland would look legitimate. Once the properties were sold and the

moneys deposited, The Assemblage would not be able to trace it to Alice or Sasha. They could go after the new owners, but anyone with that kind of money could defend themselves.

It took many days for them to make their arrangements. They would not be going on a pleasure trip and had to exchange their luggage again for smaller bags that they could carry. Since they didn't want their carry-on or any of their luggage viewed too closely—due to what was contained inside—they checked it and boarded a plane for Kazakhstan.

~ ~ ~ ~ ~

"Kazakhstan!?" Kathy exclaimed. "What was it that made you decide to go to Kazakhstan?"

Alice looked up at her wife, suddenly coming back to the present instead of her memories. Her eyes, her amazing eyes, were a shade of orange that Kathy knew should make her uncomfortable. Instead, knowing Alice as she did, they excited her. She could feel the arousal coming sharp and quick. Her breath began to fluctuate and her body responded to the unconscious invitation of danger that Alice represented. She couldn't have *not* responded had she tried....

"Kazakhstan was the key we hadn't realized before," Alice began to explain....

~The End~ K'Anne ;-P

If you have enjoyed *MEDDLESOME MALICE* you'll look forward to a sample of K'Anne Meinel's splendid and unforgettable novel:

CHAPTER ONE

Claire looked out over the endless sea. It was a pretty, deep blue-green shade which she was told was due to the unique waters of the Caribbean. As the islands they were approaching came closer, the depths would make it appear even more blue, more beautiful; many different shades of blue and green. She enjoyed the view, but not the indicators that told her she would be arriving at their destination soon. They were making for the island of Baleniesia, a small unimportant island ruled by an autocratic governor for His Majesty, the king. The governor also happened to be her father. When she reached the island she had two days to prepare for her wedding. She glanced at the man that was to be her husband and shuddered at the thought.

Sir Edmond could have been a kind man, but nature had not been kind to him. He was still afflicted with facial sores that most would have outgrown after their teens. He attempted to hide these ruptures with a beard that had never fully developed and as a result looked thin and scraggly with prominent bald spots interspersed with the sores. Ingrown hairs caused some of these sores that further made his appearance disgusting. His morose picking at the scabs did not help any, causing oils from his hands to enter the sores and cause more pus-filled ruptures. A flushed complexion, made worse from the sunburn he was sporting, did not enhance his looks in any way. Dark brown, almost black hair stood out from his scalp, chins, and cheeks. His

overly-large nose was red and veins were broken over it from drinking. His eyebrows brushed over his eyes-his only good feature. They were a twinkling brown that frequently ogled his fiancée, much to her disgust and dismay. Sir Edmond was not tall, slightly under average. He was shorter than his bride, but as he never looked her in the eye it really did not matter. Frequently, she found him looking straight down her stylishly-cut gowns, licking his lips in anticipation of their wedding night. He was constantly assuring her that she would enjoy his amorous charms. He tried frequently to discuss his past conquests with her, hoping to impress her with his well-endowed pursuits, but Claire always pleaded for her innocent ears to hear no such salacious comments. Instead of putting him off, this seemed to increase his ardor; he appeared to thrill at the thought of being Claire's first and only lover. She shivered at the thought of his sweaty hands on her body.

She quickly looked away in disgust. The prideful peacock had no idea that women found him repulsive. He seemed to think very highly of himself. He believed he was charming, rich, and handsome, despite the obvious acne on his thirty-year-old face. When she had been introduced to him by her father's London solicitor, she had frozen in the act of welcoming the man her father had written about, assuring her he was a good catch. His overly-familiar nature had disgusted her beyond his physical appearance. He quickly assured her that he would master her and show her the ways of pleasuring him. At every opportunity he groped, fondled, caressed, or pinched her body. As a result, she sported many bruises and red marks on her young, white body. She avoided him whenever she could, but being on a slow ship for the last six weeks meant she had very few places to hide. She could not always stay in her cabin. He had accosted her there once, but she had learned to keep the door locked at all times. She had taken a sudden interest in the management of the ship and to the delight of the captain and his officers had been a welcome listener to their stories, knowledge, and skills. This kept her fiancé at bay. He had no interest in the running of the ship, considering it far beneath his lofty self, but he could not interrupt the captain or his officers when they were chatting with her. He did, however, let her know he did not appreciate her talking with these men he felt were his inferiors. Unfortunately, the captain and his men were not much better in character than her fiancé, they interpreted her interest in the ship to be an interest in them as well. She had another week of fending them off before they might take liberties. Only the fact that Sir Edward was marrying the daughter of the Governor of Baleniesia kept them from doing something that would get them drawn and quartered.

Claire sighed, wishing she could change her fate, but unfortunately her father controlled it. She had met her father a total of five times in her life. He had basically abandoned her to their London servants when her mother died. Going into service of the king, he had gladly accepted the prestigious position of governor on the unheard of island of Baleniesia. He certainly did not want to be saddled with a small daughter when he was not sure of conditions on the island. Once settled, he loved his power too much to be bothered with a child, and a girl child at that. As a result, Claire had been raised by her governess,

the housekeeper, butler, and a host of maids. She had gone to prestigious schools thanks to her father's solicitors, but these gave her no home life, no love, no family. Instead she was independent; she made friends with the people who had been paid to raise her. There was no warmth other than that friendship, nothing that would be a mother-daughter or father-daughter relationship. She sighed again, thinking about what she had dreamed of for years, that she would love her husband and have beautiful children. This was unlikely with a man who looked and acted like Sir Edmund.

"Thinking of me, my dear?" he sidled up to her, making sure to touch her proprietarily by sliding an arm around her shoulder.

"No," she answered honestly, shrugging his arm off her, knowing he would think it maidenly airs. "I am thinking of what Baleniesia will look like."

That sent him off on a long and boring lecture of the island and its many benefits. It was a profitable island from sugar cane, slaves, and rum. It was strategic to His Royal Majesty's ships with a deep bay for anchoring and resupplying, which was why the governor's request for this small favor of transporting his daughter and her fiancé had been granted. Sir Edmund had gone to London himself to fetch his lovely bride. He had considered himself fortunate to obtain her hand in marriage. Her father was a lord of the realm, and with his governorship and plantations, a very wealthy man in his own right. It was definitely an advantageous marriage for Sir Edmond. It was also advantageous to him that his bride was young, nubile, and attractive. Her blonde-brown hair was beautiful and would bleach blonder in the tropical sun, if he allowed her out of their home. He thought about keeping her bound to the bedroom, perhaps tied to their bed in chains that would normally be used on slaves. He liked the idea and licked his lips repeatedly in anticipation of bedding his attractive, young fiancée. She would be a good bed partner he was sure of that. He would teach her all the things that he liked.

Claire listened with only half an ear, nodding occasionally as her mind drifted. Sir Edmund would never notice. He was so self-involved giving her an education on something he felt so superior about, that he never considered that she was not interested in what he had to say. Unfortunately, he felt himself superior on many subjects and his droning on tended to bore his listeners. He never noticed, too impressed with his own knowledge to acknowledge theirs. Claire looked out at the waves, praying to the heavens for a reprieve from this obnoxious and disgusting man.

The heavens answered.

"Sail ho," a call came from the eagle's nest, a spot manned by one of the sailors up on one of the high spars.

Everyone on deck except Sir Edmund looked immediately to where the man pointed over the horizon. Faintly, the tall spars of another ship could be seen. It took some time, but as it began to creep up over the horizon, they could see it clearly. By then Edmund had finally become aware that his captive audience was looking elsewhere and turned to look himself. "Do not worry, my dear, I will protect you!" he assured his fiancée, who he assumed was frightened, as he took advantage of the moment to put his arm around her again.

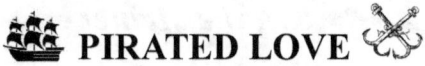 

Claire leaned forward slightly so his arm dropped off her shoulder and wondered aloud, "I wonder if they are a merchantman's ship?"

"I am sure if they are, they are unimportant to His Majesty's business," he said pompously, annoyed that she had once again avoided his touch.

They all watched as it slowly and majestically made its way towards them, apparently on a course that would intersect their own. The captain and his officers discussed its intentions and a spyglass was brought out to try to identify the ship, which apparently was not flying a flag. It was soon obvious that the ship was larger than their own, its four masts huge against the background of the sky. It cut through the waves easily as it sailed along, its huge and graceful lines making little effort as its beautiful, white sails filled with wind. As it came closer, its black appearance seemed as ominous as its silent and huge presence.

A shout went up from the captain after consulting his officers. "It is Black Betty!" he called to his crew and immediately demanded they get the most out of their own sails to get far away from this famous pirate's ship. "Mason, break out arms for all," he called to his arms master.

Claire felt curiously excited. She had heard all sorts of tales from the captain and his officers, but the ones that seemed to fascinate her the most were those told about pirates. Black Betty had several tales that had intrigued and delighted Claire. She knew that she should not approve of piracy, but the fact that this ship was commanded by a woman had thrilled her. She had listened avidly when they talked about the rogue captain of the pirate ship. It was rumored that she took men *and* women as lovers, and she freed men from jail for her vagabond crew which made them exceedingly loyal. She shared her treasure with them and owned an island somewhere that was made of gold. She had no compunction killing men or women; she fought better than most men. She had never been caught and brought to justice and no one could find where she hid, what happened to her captives, or the treasures that she plundered. The outrageous tales about her were probably false, but then Claire was sure they had grown with time and boredom of the men who grudgingly respected the woman for doing what she wanted.

A curious sense of expectation took over the crew as they all came on deck to fight off the rapidly overtaking ship, its larger countenance causing the captain and his officers to sweat as they swore and ordered the men to take on more sail, to get them going faster than the other ship. It was to no avail as the other ship fired across their bow, an obvious request for them to stop. The captain ignored it, swearing at the other ship, the sound carried across the waters as it overtook them. Grappling hooks were repelled as it came alongside.

Claire stood back against the doors that led down to the hold, for once letting Sir Edmund hold her around the shoulders. In her case, it was more because she did not notice, in his case, because of his real fear. The bulk of the doors behind her felt good against her back as she watched the pirates swing aboard.

"Repel them," the captain shouted, unnecessarily.

Claire watched as the defenders of her ship shot unsuccessfully, oftentimes the gun they were using misfiring or not firing at all and their accuracy was awful. The clash of swords was loud as the pirates

swarmed across as the two ships crashed together, the grappling hooks now successful in holding the two ships side by side. The men fought desperately, bravely, and Claire did not know much about sword fighting, but even her untutored eyes could see that the pirates were far superior in skill as they quickly disarmed and sometimes killed the battling sailors. The fighting was ferocious, sweaty, and quick; the pirates were soon victorious.

Claire watched amazed as a woman came across the small gap between the two ships. She was dressed as a man with her hair flowing madly about her shoulders and back, its red gleam shining in the light of the sun, bright gold earrings hanging from both her ears. She looked wild and untamed as she walked up to the captain who was held between two swarthy-looking men who had never washed, were naked from the waist up, and sported odd little shoes that had tips that curled up. She wore two swords crisscrossed over her back, her hair nearly hiding them in its length, but the handles were just over her shoulders so she could grab them as needed. Right now, she was holding a sword in her hand from the belt at her waist.

"Do you yield?" a very effeminate voice sternly asked.

The captain spat at her and she looked at the spittle that hit the deck of the captured ship. Her eyes narrowed ominously and with a little nod of her head the two men who held the captain began to strip him despite his protests and then proceeded to throw him into the ocean over the edge of his ship.

"Well, lookee what we have here," a voice spoke close to Claire's ear and she turned to see a disgusting man with brown, fuzzy teeth

leering at her as he reached for her. In the clash of the fight, she and Sir Edmund had been overlooked and now the pirates were systematically looking for anyone hiding or for hidden loot, and had discovered her. He grabbed her away from Sir Edmund easily, who curiously did not protest. "Hey, boys, looks like we gets some fun!" he grinned and laughed evilly as several men began to pinch, grab, and feel up the protesting woman.

"No, *no*, NO!" she screeched, as they began to tear at her clothes and bear her down to the deck of the ship. She saw one of the men lower his trousers and she saw a pole of white flesh swelling from it. She looked away helplessly as she tried to kick and struggle, but was held down easily by the lustful men who pulled her skirts up and ripped off her drawers, touching her where no one had ever touched, not even she, other than through a washcloth. She screamed, which seemed to egg on the men. Glancing over at her fiancé who had sworn to defend her, she saw him easily being held by two men, but also watching avidly. She screamed loud and long as the man kneeled between her spread legs.

"Halt!" the feminine voice commanded.

The man grabbed her hips as he went to thrust between her legs.

A sword tip slashed down in front of his lust-filled eyes and stopped just short of his erect cock. He froze in the act of raping the young woman and looked up at the angry green eyes of his captain. Her intent was clear, either he halted his act or she would slice off his manhood. Knowing her as he did, he shrunk before all their eyes and quickly

tucked it away, standing up with his head hung low. She raised his chin with her sword tip.

"Can you listen, Johann?" she asked, ominously.

"Sorry, Captain, I's caught up. She is a prize," he defended himself weakly.

She glanced down on the deck at the sprawled body of the young woman she had just saved from being ravished. The blouse of her gown was torn open and her breasts were on view to all the lustful looks of her men and the crew of the other ship who could see from their own kneeling positions. She admired the view herself for a moment. "So she is, but she is more valuable to us as a hostage. Are you and I going to have problems over this, Johann?" she asked, in a cultured voice that brooked no argument.

"No, ma'am, er, sir," he stuttered, knowing she would not hesitate to kill him where he stood.

She smiled as she lowered the razor-sharp sword and ordered, "Cover her up!" Looking around at the sailors of the captured ship, she spied the still struggling Sir Edmund who was swearing and protesting over his capture.

"I am Sir Edmund Fitzhugh! You have no right...!" he was shouting.

"They will not understand you," she yelled over him in a perfect English accent and he subsided, relieved to have someone who might finally understand him as the two dirty men had not answered in English. Instead they spoke some gibberish he had no hope of understanding as he struggled to be released from them and they swore at him in their own languages.

"Finally! I DEMAND that you release me immediately. I am Sir Edmund..." he began, pompously, but trailed off as she swiftly brought her sword up to his unprotected throat to get his full attention.

"You are NOTHING now. I am in charge here and you are at my mercy. If I choose to sell you as a slave or drown you here, it is MY choice and not your own. So do be good enough to be quiet while I decide what to do with you." She turned away from the disgusting man whose eyes were nearly popping out of his sockets at the sword.

"Strip the ship," she ordered, in several different languages. It was obvious she knew them too, as she effortlessly gave the order.

Each of the captured sailors was given the opportunity to tell what they knew about their own ship as the pirates searched them for weapons and valuables. Many of the pirates knew many different languages, or at least a smattering, so they could ask their English prisoners questions. The pirates began to take their plunder across to their own ship. They used the labor of their captives to bring up the booty from the hold. Anyone who resisted was stripped and thrown immediately into the water as an example to any who would not work. They were watched to see that they did not try to again get on board or on the pirates' own ship. It is a helpless man who is naked and floating in the ocean, attempting to keep afloat or, as a couple of the men were, holding on to the ship as best they could at the water line, waiting for the decision of the pirate captain and their fate. They did not hold out

much hope; the captain was not known for her generosity to captives if she even bothered to take any of them.

"Take her to my cabin," she ordered one of the men, indicating Claire who was now wrapped and shivering in a blanket. He nodded as he solicitously helped the woman up.

"Is that Black Betty?" Claire asked, as they made their way to the larger ship.

The man nodded as he pushed his way past other pirates and men working to transfer booty and supplies as the smaller ship was slowly stripped of all usable rigging, supplies, and cargo.

He showed her to a luxuriously furnished apartment with a large set of windows and an actual bed instead of the normal bunks that were found on a ship. This bed, Claire could see, was bolted to the floor as any furniture on a ship normally was to prevent it becoming a nuisance in bad weather. Men had been known to be crushed from moving cargo or gear caused by the battering that waves gave a ship. "If I were you, mademoiselle," he began, in a French accent. "I would do *ANYTHING* the capitan asks of you." He locked her inside and Claire shivered in a chair, refusing to lie on the bed, not knowing her fate. The little she had gleaned from what the captain had said was that she was valuable and they would be using her as a hostage. She wondered if her father would pay? She looked around the cabin at the shelves of books with a thin rail set up on the ledges to keep the books from falling off them. There were several cabinets and she wondered if they contained clothing or other personal items, but she did not explore. There was a large table bolted to the floor in the middle of the room

with an odd little lip of wood around the edge and she realized this was so the dishes would not slide off onto the floor when they ate meals. A bench stood bolted to the floor on each side of the table and two chairs, one on each end, both elegantly appointed and plush. There were odd little hooks above head level in the walls and in the ceiling rafters, and she wondered at these as she glanced around.

She finally stopped shivering enough that she stood up to look out the large window along the back of the apartment. She could look out over the smaller ship as the pirate ship had shifted forward a little in the current. She could clearly see the men who were moving cargo and booty to the pirate ship. The sailors were working to save their own lives for they knew the pirates would not hesitate to kill anyone reluctant to work. She could see where Edmund had been stripped down naked in front of the pirate captain. His white body was even uglier than his face. It was scrawny and the black hairs covered most of it, almost as a pelt to make up for the sparse facial hair. The little worm between his legs caught her attention with all his bragging. This was going to enthrall her? As little as she knew about men, after seeing the horrible thing that was the pirate's manhood she instinctively knew that this little insipid thing would have been disappointing despite his boasts. She watched as the captain struck the man with her own fists repeatedly in the jaw, using both hands on each side of his face, then one to his stomach. As he bent over, she kneed him swiftly in the face causing his nose to spurt blood. With a flick of her head, she indicated to throw him overboard. Wiping her hands as though she had dirtied them, she looked around and then suddenly up, catching Claire looking

down on the scene, before smiling insolently and turning deliberately away.

The transfer of their booty was achieved in a relatively short time. The pirates were thorough and took nothing that did not have value. There was no point in hauling damaged goods or something with weight that would give them no profit. They stripped sails, took the extras, even fittings and hardware. The captain and her pirate crew left the long-boats for the crew of the British ship before going across to their own ship and unhooking the grappling hooks. The sailors who had cooperated were left aboard to decide the fate of those floating in the ocean as the pirate ship sailed away. Left with no sails, the ship was useless and they got out the long boats to put in the water. The pirate captain had left them three day's rations and they were going to try to row to the nearest populated islands.

It was quite dark when Claire heard the door unlock and open. "Put it there." She heard the curiously feminine voice of the captain and turned over from where she lay on the couch beside the window to see a pirate bring in a tray of food. Its aroma preceded it and Claire's stomach rumbled. It smelled delicious, whatever it was. The pirate left almost immediately, bowing slightly to the captain who looked around and spotted Claire on the couch. Going to some of the lamps, she produced a sulfur match and lighted them one by one to bring light to the room. She walked over to Claire.

"What is your name?" she asked in her upper crust British accent, which amazed Claire.

"Claire Von Hagen, but my family and friends call me Claire," she said quietly, wondering what would happen now.

"Well, Lady Von Hagen, your fiancé was most forthcoming with information," the captain told her, but did not continue telling with what information. "Come. Eat. I am sure you want to know what I have in mind for you," she offered, as her hand indicated the food on the table and her other hand was held out to help her rise from the settee. Claire appreciated the courtesy, but found it odd that a woman dressed as a man would offer it.

They sat down to a delicious stew of meat and vegetables, wholesome fare for a ship, with biscuits that were flaky and bug-free and apparently fairly fresh. Claire had not eaten this well since she had boarded her own ship and she ate heartily, the food wonderful and filling. The captain was amused as she watched her captive eat with gusto, but then she ate just as much. Claire noted the captain was fastidious, using a napkin on her lap, her pinky finger outstretched as she sipped at tea or wine, unconsciously feminine in her eating habits. Claire herself still had the blanket wrapped around her torn dress and felt outclassed at this table despite the captain being dressed in men's clothing.

The captain allowed her to fill her belly before talking to her. "Now, we will not be getting anywhere near your father's island to demand a ransom. This could take months, depending on your father," she explained. "You have a choice though."

Claire listened appreciatively at the civil tone of the captain. She was being treated with respect and courtesy and had nothing to prepare her for what the captain further told her.

"You can service my crew as the only female available to them, or you can service me for the duration of your stay." She waited for this to sink in to her captive's mind.

Claire's eyes opened wide making her look like a doe as the meaning of the words penetrated her mind. The warm and delicious food had lulled her into a state where she had thought she would be safe and protected until her ransom was paid. The thought of men raping her over and over again certainly did not appeal. She had thought the captain, being a woman, she would be safe from any physical harm. She had no idea what two women did together; she could not begin to understand that part of the captain's offer. "Service you?" she asked, hesitantly, as though to clarify the proposition.

The captain smiled. It made her striking face beautiful. Her red hair was tied back now, but it still flowed down her back and her darkly tanned features looked very attractive in the lamp light. "Aye, I am sure you do not know what that entails, but I assure you I enjoy both men and women's bodies, and you will enjoy my attentions more than you will my crew's," she guaranteed her.

"I can take care of your apartment for you...?" she began, hoping against sinking hope that the woman did not mean what she was implying. She remembered the warning she had received from the pirate earlier, to do whatever the captain demanded.

The captain laughed. "Nay, I assure you, I do not mean that. I mean you will have sexual relations with me," she said properly, in her upper crust tones. There was a hint of another accent though, not completely British.

There it was, spelled out for Claire to understand. She had a choice of being raped repeatedly by the crew-they would not kill her, she knew, because of the ransom-or succumbing to the captain. She had heard that sailor crews were notoriously dirty and unclean and had diseases. She had no idea of what she could easily catch, but having relations with another female? It was a sin, was it not? She thought hard, back to the teachings of her church, and she was sure it was a sin to sleep with someone of the same gender. Sleeping with the crew, even one of them, would dirty her, ruin her in the eyes of the church, her fiancé, and her father. She shuddered at the thought of one of them, much less the many, touching her. The alternative was death and she had no chance of dying, that she could tell; she was too valuable. She reluctantly nodded, numbly, resignedly, realizing her fate was not her own, and feeling helpless again.

"I want you to tell me exactly, so there is no misunderstanding between us," the captain stated, looking at her closely as she examined the pretty blonde's countenance.

"I will service you for the duration of my stay," Claire said quietly, almost in a whisper, horrified at what she had just agreed to.

TO BE CONTINUED...

About the Author

K'Anne Meinel is the BEST SELLING author of LAWYERED, REPRESENTED, SMALL TOWN ANGEL, BLOWN AWAY, and SAPPHIC SURFER as well as several other books including her first SHIPS which was written over the course of two weeks. A gypsy at heart she has lived in many locations and plans to continue doing that. Videos of several of her books are available on You Tube outlining some of the locations of her books and telling a little bit more…giving the readers insight into her mind as she created these wonderful stories.

K'Anne Meinel pronounced Kay Ann My Null, is an American author born and raised in Wisconsin. While she has lived in Central and Southern California, many of her stories have taken on locations from and around the states.

K'Anne professes to write books that she would like to read and through her novels, novellas, and her short stories has grown into a writer who is willing to expand her horizons. She fearlessly steps out of her comfort zone in order to allow the reader to taste through her words, experiences of her life.

Her first book SHIPS was written in 2003, but bits of it were re-written off and on for the next eight years before she self-published it and then was approached by a publisher. Short stories joined her 'bill of fare' in 2011 purely as a personal mind exercise. 2011 also saw the beginning of a series of books which all include 'Malice' in their titles. This deliciously gripping series leaves the reader suspended, starving, and craving more. Now with over eighty titles to her credit, including various translations, K'Anne can truly claim to be an established author.

Several years ago K'Anne created Shadoe Publishing in order to showcase her books under a publishing logo and house. Many outlets will not accept independently self-published books. Shadoe Publishing met that need and allowed K'Anne to use skills in running a company that she had acquired over twenty-five years with running other companies. In other words, to market and showcase new and upcoming authors. Shadoe Publishing has expanded since its inception and includes more than a couple dozen other authors who have used K'Anne time and skills under the Shadoe Publishing brand to promote their works. K'Anne has no intention of being the 'biggest' publisher of LGBT works, but she does intend to be the most supportive and the most successful in the unique atmosphere that she has created for her authors.

K'Anne is the Mistress of sarcasm, double entendre, and has a wicked tongue-in-cheek humor that many find addictive. She has a way with words. Her descriptions become visions in your mind. Her words fuel your imagination. Befriend or 'like' her on Facebook, Twitter and keep up with her books, stories, and career. There is sure to be something you'll enjoy. Feel free to email comments, suggestions, or advice.

~ Because a publisher should stand behind their authors~

Among the majestic shoreline of the Central Coast of California lies a secret...Leah Van Heusen finds a hidden staircase....

The ancient house she finds among the overgrown foliage is amazing...and eerie, most wouldn't even step a foot closer but she is intrigued and feels drawn to the old mansion....

Leah finds more than she bargains for after seeking out the owner and purchasing the entire estate for a dollar. As she starts to restore it, she finds out who her real friends are, she also finds out who her family really is...What's a few ghosts between friends?

Between repairs, upgrades, and finding out the houses secrets, Leah has her hands full. Finding out her sexuality and dating is the least of her worries. As her beloved dream of an Inn becomes reality she finds it suddenly in jeopardy, who will kill for it or the immense fortune that she has found?

www.shadoepublishing.com

~ Because a publisher should stand behind their authors~

What do you do when you meet someone who changes everything you know about love and passion?

Paige Harlow is a good girl. She's always known where she was going in life: top grades, an ivy league school, a medical degree, regular church attendance, and a happy marriage to a man. So falling in love with her gorgeous roommate and best friend Alyssa Torres is no small crisis. Alyssa is chasing demons of her own, a medical condition that makes her an outcast and a family dysfunctional to the point of disintegration make her a questionable choice for any stable relationship. But Paige's heart is no longer her own. She must now battle the prejudices of her family, friends, and church and come to peace with her new sexuality before she can hope to win the affections of the woman of her dreams. But will love be enough?

~ Because a publisher should stand behind their authors~

As I watch the wormhole start to close, I make one last desperate plea ...
"Please? Please don't make me do this?" I whisper.
"You're almost out of time, Lily. Please, just let go?"
I look down at the control panel. I know what I have to do.

Lilith Madison is captain of the Phoenix, a spaceship filled with an elite crew and travelling through the Delta Gamma Quadrant. Their mission is mankind's last hope for survival.

But there is a killer on board. One who kills without leaving a trace and seems intent on making sure their mission fails. With the ship falling apart and her crew being ruthlessly picked off one by one, Lilith must choose who to trust while tracking down the killer before it's too late.

"A suspenseful...exciting...thrilling whodunit adventure in space...discover the shocking truth about what's really happening on the Phoenix" (Clarion)

When Delaney Delacroix is called to locate a missing girl, she never plans on getting caught up with a human trafficking investigation or with the local witch. Meeting with Raelin Montrose changes her life in so many ways that Delaney isn't sure that this isn't destiny.

Raelin Montrose is a practicing Wiccan, and when the ley lines that run under her home tell her that someone is coming, she can't imagine that she was going to solve a mystery and find the love of her life at the same time.

~ Because a publisher should stand behind their authors~

A Children's Novel for ages 8-11

Horse crazy Lily, eleven years old with two out-loud-and-proud mothers, is plump and clumsy. Her mothers say she's too young to ride horses, she can't seem to get anything right in class, and bullies torment her on the playground. Alone and lonely, how will she ever survive the mean girls of Hardyvale Elementary's fifth-grade?

Across the room Clara sits still as a statue, never volunteering or raising her hand. To avoid the bullying that is Lily's daily life she answers only in a whisper with her head down, desperate to keep her family's secret that she has two fathers.

Then one day Clara makes a brave move that changes the girls' lives forever. She passes a note to Lily asking to meet secretly at lunch time. As they share cupcakes she explains about her in-the-closet dads. Both girls are relieved to finally have a friend, especially one who understands about living in a rainbow family.

Life gets better. As their friendship deepens and their families grow close, their circle of friends expand. The girls even volunteer together at the local animal shelter. Everything is great, until old lies and blackmail catch up with them. Can Lily and her mothers rescue Clara's family from disaster? Or will Lily lose her first and best friend?

~ Because a publisher should stand behind their authors~

Amelia Gittens had the credit of being the first and only woman thus far in the United States military of being a sniper in combat, made possible by being in the Military Police unit of the crack 10th Mountain Infantry Division. After retirement she joins the City of New York Police Department, and suddenly finds herself involved in a suspect shooting incident which soon encroaches upon her entire life. In order to protect her therapist who has been targeted as a revenge killing, Amelia takes on the responsibility as if she was still in the Army, treating it as a tactical maneuver.

~ Because a publisher should stand behind their authors~

When U.S. Marine Dakota McKnight returned home from her third tour in Operation Iraqi Freedom, she carried more baggage than the gear and dress blues she had deployed with. A vicious rocket-propelled grenade attack on her base left her best friend dead and Dakota physically and emotionally wounded. The marine who once carried herself with purpose and confidence, has returned broken and haunted by the horrors of war. When she returns to the civilian world, life is not easy, but with the help of her therapist, Janie, she is barely managing to hold her life together...then she meets Beth.

Beth Kendrick is an American history college professor. She is as straight-laced as they come, until Dakota enters her life, that is. Will her children understand what she is going through? Will she take a chance on the broken marine or decide to wait for the perfect someone to come along?

Time is on your side, they say, unless there is a dark, sinister evil at work. Is their love strong enough to hold these two people together? Will the love of a good woman help Dakota find the path to recovery? Or is she doomed to a life of inner turmoil and destruction that knows no end?

www.shadoepublishing.com

An abused and bullied teenager is suddenly granted great and terrible powers by an ancient goddess. Each step towards womanhood is shaped by her new abilities, as is the woman she will become. Devil or angel, which will she be? Will the woman who chases her ever know for sure?

Both men tried to shoot her then, and the two women were stunned at the speed with which she moved. Penny charged straight at the gunmen then dove under their fire. Spinning on her back she kicked the legs from under one man, and as he fell, she kicked the gun from the other man's hand. Spinning back to the first man she saw the gun barrel moving toward her, and she lashed out with her foot. Her boot crushed his skull and she rolled to her feet to grab the last man in a neck lock. A quick twist and he lay lifeless in her arms.

She let him fall, as, breathing deeply, she came down off combat mode. "Are you ladies all right?" she asked as she untied the ropes that held the older woman.

"Who are you?" asked the old woman fearfully, as she pulled the tape from her mouth.

"They call me Lady Blue," smiled Penny as she helped the woman to stand.

"What are you?" It was the younger woman who spoke.

"Cold, hungry, dead tired, and covered in blue war paint," giggled Penny as she released the older woman's arm. She turned and began to search the bodies.

~ Because a publisher should stand behind their authors~

Sadie is in love for the first time with Sparrow when a tragedy tears them apart...will revenge finally reunite the pair and will they be together forever?

An E-Book first by Wolfie Stone

*If you have enjoyed this book and the others listed here Shadoe
Publishing is always looking for first, second, or third time
authors. Please check out our website @
www.shadoepublishing.com
For information or to contact us @
shadoepublishing@gmail.com.*

*We may be able to help you make your dreams of becoming
a published author come true.*

www.ingramcontent.com/pod-product-compliance
Lightning Source LLC
Chambersburg PA
CBHW070936130626
46555CB00001B/464